MARY JEMISON
WHITE WOMAN OF THE SENECA

MARY JEMISON
WHITE WOMAN OF THE SENECA

A NOVEL BY
RAYNA M. GANGI

EPILOGUE BY PETER JEMISON

CLEAR LIGHT PUBLISHERS
SANTA FE

Clear Light Publishers, 823 Don Diego, Santa Fe, New Mexico

Library of Congress Cataloging in Publication Data
Gangi, Rayna M., 1950–
    Mary Jemison: white woman of the Seneca by Rayna M. Gangi; epilogue by Peter Jemison.
    p. cm.
    ISBN 0-940666-57-X (cloth): $22.95
    ISBN 0-940666-58-8 (pbk.): $12.95
    1. Jemison, Mary, 1743–1833—Fiction. 2. Indian captivities—Genesee River Valley (Pa. and N.Y.)—Fiction. 3. Genesee River Valley (Pa. and N.Y.)—History—Fiction. 4. New York (State)—History—Fiction. 5. Seneca Indians—Fiction. I. Title.
PS3557.A513M37   1995
813'.54—dc20   94–43546
                                                                        CIP

Cover photograph by Marcia Keegan.
Drawing on back cover and page ii, *Longhouse*, by Michael Otterson.

Printed in the United States of America

ACKNOWLEDGEMENTS

The author gratefully acknowledges the following: The Buffalo and Erie County Historical Society, SUNY at Buffalo, and The University of Rochester for their help in the research of this book. Also thanks to Ruth, Shirley, Sue and Mom for reading and responding so quickly. A special thanks to Julia for her patience and support.

PART I

1

Mary Jemison felt the cool, crisp earth sift through her cal-
loused fingers as she gently covered the last of the six corn
seeds. She knew this harvest would be better than any in the fifteen years they'd been in America. Spring was early and the earth
felt ready for seed. Her father, Tom, a boisterous, commanding
Irishman, had cleared the land himself, praying at each meal that
the settling of America also would confirm his homestead.

To Mary, each seed of corn was a member of her family
that demanded special care to ensure its survival. She covered
the seeds with a tenderness she knew the Earth didn't need.
She respected the land, nurtured it, even scolded it with loving
firmness if it didn't respond as she thought it should. Truly she
felt nature was hers to hold. The wind was a refreshing breath
from God and the trees of oak, elm, maple, and pine were her
blanket. The thick forest that surrounded the Jemisons' large
farm was, she was sure, a gift from God to be wandered, embraced and revered.

The weather was changing and Mary could feel life bursting from the ground. She thought change was good. The
changing of seasons caressed her white skin, molding it,
smoothing it, preparing it for womanhood. The changes in
her body pleased her. She felt the tides within her ebb and
flow with the moon, sometimes crushing her into sadness,
often filling her with joyful tears. Life was exciting. She never
wanted that to change.

She was short for fifteen, only five feet tall and built more like her mother, though she earnestly tried to be strong like her father. Still, she enjoyed the admiration of those around her and was known to blush when complimented for her beauty. She often checked her reflection in the river that cut through the hills and she smiled at the woman who budded before her.

The sound of her brother John's ax broke the stillness of the spring morning. He was the oldest, taller than his father, but most like him, with a temper that blasted at all who opposed him, but a respect for his family that prevented any outburst. To Mary he was a cougar, always ready to spring on his prey. Sometimes she feared him; often she didn't understand him. He was John, wild and angry, and her brother, caring and loyal.

Jesse was younger, the first Jemison born in America, and was as tempered as its valleys. He was quiet and sensitive, always alert to the needs of those around him. It was Jesse who went without sleep for days as he nursed a sick lamb back to health. It was Jesse who knew when it was time to only listen so that Mary could rage at her loneliness or sing of a new daydream.

Though Mary loved all her family, Jesse was her favorite friend and Papa was her pillar.

"Trust in the Lord and trust in me," Tom always said.

Mary almost sang those words as she gathered her remaining seeds and skipped the long path to the barn.

Ripping branches and crashing limbs choked the freshness of the day as John's ax finished its job, and Mary could hear Tom's deep voice calling out from the barn.

"Good job, lads! Good job!"

He was proud of his family and of his land. He hummed an Irish tune made up by his mother as he waited with open arms for his sons to return.

He put an arm around each and walked them toward the house.

"Tomorrow we'll be clearin' and plowin' that new field.

Your Mama and baby Matthew will be eating corn pone through the winter. I thank ya, lads."

"Why, those trees cut as easy as pone," said John. "We're proud to chop 'em."

"Just the same," answered Tom. "The good Lord put some of those trees in our path to test our strength and our will. Without you boys your Mama and I might well be on the William and Mary, sailin' back to face the wrath of Ireland." Tom's face hardened as he momentarily remembered the religious strife in his homeland.

"Was it a big farm you had then, Pa?" Jesse always asked about Ireland when he knew his father needed it.

"Not as big as this . . . or as fine," said Tom. "But, aye, it was a good one. Sometimes I wish we had stayed." Tom drew in his breath and expanded his chest as he surveyed the land around him. "This is our home now. The hills of Pennsylvania. Green and strong and waiting for new life."

Mary approached with a smile and Tom, as always, stretched out his arms to greet her.

"And here you are darlin' daughter. The best cornplanter this side of the sea!"

Mary hugged him tightly, savoring the smell of chopped wood and oiled leather that seemed to always float from his clothes.

"You're the best, Papa. I just learned it from you."

"But you learned wrong," interrupted Jesse. "You plant too slow . . . countin' and pettin' those seeds . . . like they was babies or something."

Tom smiled. "Now, Jesse. Your sister has a special feel for the land. The Lord gave her a certain patience, a certain way of seeing things."

"Sure. One . . . two . . . three . . . ," Jesse mimicked.

Tom squeezed Mary closer to him, shielding her from Jesse's teasing. She didn't mind Jesse. She knew he loved farming as much as she did. He often wanted to join her in the

11

fields, but Tom gave him other chores, hunting and tanning. Work he thought more necessary for his growth to manhood.

"That's her way of keepin' up her schooling," Tom said. "You learn from your Ma, and John here learned on the ship, countin' the days 'til your sister was born. The Lord makes each of us learn a special way."

John and Jesse nodded respectfully and ran ahead to the house. Tom and Mary walked slowly, arm in arm, Mary stopped her father before they got to the door. She didn't want the others to hear.

"Papa, I don't really count the seeds to practice."

Tom just smiled and listened, stroking the red-gold hair of the daughter he adored.

"I see each seed as one of us . . . and I name them. Then, when I see the corn growing and it fills the fields waving and tossin' with the breeze, I know we're all together . . . and safe."

Tom looked at her with a father's pride and paused to check the sun's position in the sky. It was time for prayers and a meal and, though his time with Mary was always precious to him, he was also very prompt and very strict about giving thanks to his God.

They entered the large house to the smell of frying corn pone, the greasy smoke swirling up to the double loft and clinging to the shaved skins on the windows. Two year old Matthew sat in the cradle that Jesse carved from a fallen tree. Jane Jemison, her long, fiery red hair falling across her small and bony shoulders, scurried back and forth from the large wooden table to the open fireplace. She knew her husband's rules of promptness and she never failed to please him. Three times a day his meals were ready. Three times a day she gathered the family for prayer.

Mary trusted their love for each other and almost envied their closeness. She was fifteen. It was time she found someone to marry. But she wanted a man like her Pa, a man of the woods, a protector. They had friends in the surrounding hills and valleys, but they were miles apart. No one close enough to the farm had a son old enough for her. She was afraid she'd die alone, an old woman without a family, and she often dreamed of a stranger who would love her and marry her, be with her forever. She was always the last one at the table and the least prepared to lead the family in prayer. Jane warned her that daydreaming could be sinful and no amount of dreaming could give her strength, and she was steadfast in her rules for Mary. She must always be a lady, standing straight and steady. She must study her English and her prayers and be ready to serve whatever man chose her to be his wife.

"It's time to thank the Lord for our day," Jane said after the meal. "Mary, it's your turn to lead."

Mary got the bible from its place on the mantle. She always thought it strange that her mother wanted the book of God kept on the mantle beneath a squirrel gun that her Papa called the weapon of death.

She checked the rest of the corn pone that fried while the fire was still hot, then took her place in front of the fireplace as the family joined hands in a circle. Jane took baby Matt's hand and stood erect, signalling Mary to do the same. They all bowed their heads and waited for Mary to slowly read the prayer.

"Our Father, who be in Heaven. Ye name be hallowed. Thy Kingdom will come and Thy will shall be done on Earth, as it be in Heaven. . . ."

The sound of an approaching horse startled Mary into silence and all eyes rose to the thick oak door. Strangers who came without announcing themselves with a holler or a whistle always brought trouble or bad news. Tom patted Jane's clenched hand and turned to the entrance.

"No!" shouted Jane. "Tom, no! We heard no one call out!"

Tom stopped and Jane grabbed the bible from Mary's hand. She held it close to her heaving chest and, at the same time, seemed to shield Matthew from everyone around him.

Mary watched John straighten his muscular stance, ready for any intruder. Jesse was calmer, more passive. He seemed to smile at everyone's tension.

The sound of the horse got louder as it came closer. They heard its abrupt halt outside the door and all stood silently waiting.

Suddenly the large door slammed open. Jeb Wheeler, a neighboring farmer, charged into the room. He was frightened, winded. Though the chill of spring still hovered outside, the sweat from his hard and fast ride drenched his clothes and dripped from his bushy eyebrows.

"Tom! Jane!" He screamed. "They're a comin'!"

Tom let down his guard and Jane released her hold on Matthew. They knew Jeb was an anxious man who seemed afraid of everything. He had come to them before when he believed the forest was on fire. Tom was burning branches, clearing a new plot of land when Jeb saw the smoke. He gathered his family and raced to Tom's house to tell him to clear out, only to find Tom calmly tending a fire.

"Did you hear me, Tom?" Wheeler continued. "They burned the Johnsons out, killed the whole family!"

Mary moved to the shelter of her father's side while John reached for the gun above the mantle. Tom looked at him and firmly motioned for him to put the rifle back.

"We won't be needin' that, son," he said.

John reluctantly obeyed, but kept a hand on the ready knife he carried on his hip.

"Jeb, You need to calm yourself," said Tom. "Come in. Sit."

"I'll fetch you some water, Mr. Wheeler," said Jane. "You must be thirsty after your hard ride."

Jeb was dazed. "What? Water? Tom, it's the Shawnee! And the French! They burned out the Johnsons. We got to get . . ."

Tom calmly interrupted. "No, no, no. Sit, Jeb. Or stand and join us."

He turned to Mary and motioned for her to continue with

14

the prayer. Mary took the bible from Jane, checking her mother's solemn eyes for any sign of fear. Her mother was stoic, politely calm. "Give us daily our bread," she read. "And forgive us for all our wrongs. . . ."

Wheeler grabbed Tom's arm and tried to whisper to him while Mary was reading. "Tom, don't ya hear?"

"Hush, Man!" Tom never let anyone interrupt a prayer. "We're givin' our thanks. Talkin' to our Lord."

Wheeler knew Tom's devotion from the part-time preaching he did for the neighbors. He gently rose and stood beside him, bowing his head with the family.

Mary continued. ". . . And let us forgive those that wrong us. Leave us not to be tempted and save us from all evil."

A deafening silence filled the room mixing with the smell from the now burned corn pone. Mary slowly raised her eyes and looked at her family. While they waited for her to finish they stood rigid and detached. Swirls of smoke from the fireplace circled them and Mary felt the coldness of their fear. She watched her father, eyes closed and silent, and wondered how his belief in God could be so strong. It seemed he relied on God for everything, for every ounce of his strength. She closed her eyes for a moment and silently asked God to keep them safe.

"Amen."

The family answered in unison. "Amen."

Mary replaced the bible and waited for Tom's satisfied nod of approval. Then Tom sat Jeb down across from him at the table and lowered his voice to a reassuring and calming tone.

"Now. Tell us, Lad. What is it you've been hearing? Tell us your story."

Jeb looked around the room nervously. Everyone but John was smiling, waiting for him to speak. He swallowed hard. He didn't want them to think he was foolish. He loved them. He had gone through many of the same struggles they had. They were neighbors in a land where neighbors disappeared with each new day; neighbors who died from sickness or at the hands of strangers; neighbors who believed in freedom. They had moved west from Philadelphia and talked of their dreams. Philadelphia was the beginning of a new world, and they were its new people. He wanted them to listen, to understand the danger.

"Well, 'bout two nights ago," he began, "the Johnsons . . . you know. They live some ways on the other side of Marsh Creek? Well, a bunch of French soldiers and a handful of Shawnee surprised old Jeremy. You could see the smoke all the way through the trees to my brother Bob's place."

Tom leaned back and tapped his upper lip with his index finger. Mary knew her father was trying to be serious with Wheeler. He always tapped his lip, as if he was reminding himself not to smile. But Mary felt confused. Wheeler's story sounded real and frightening to her. She listened to Tom with a daughter's faith that he would keep them safe.

"I know where you mean. That's some ways off. Don't know the Johnsons to be the kind of people to rile the Indians, though." He winked to Jane. "Are ya sure they weren't burnin' some brush, Jeb?"

Wheeler interrupted quickly. "As soon as we saw the smoke me and Bob took off to see what happened. It was nothin' no body would like to witness. The smoke was a mixture of wood and flesh. . . ." He stopped and looked at Jane and Mary.

"No need to protect the women," said Tom. "They've heard stories like this before."

Tom seemed more serious now. His game with Wheeler was over. He listened intently as Wheeler continued.

"Well, it looked like the Johnsons been cut up like pieces of squash pie." Wheeler's voice was shaky and Mary thought she saw a tear in his eye. She felt sorry for him.

"Their bodies were hung on poles . . . turned to ashes. The house and barn was cinders. Nothin' left. Except the cornfield. They didn't lay a hoof on that. It was as clean and smooth as a fresh grave. Took all their food, though."

16

Wheeler stopped and lowered his head and John quickly reached for the gun. Jesse's face whitened from fear, but he automatically moved to John's side to do whatever his brother told him.

"Pa, don't you think it's time to get goin'?" John said, almost demanding a response. "Me and Jesse could get up on the barn, so's we can see 'em comin'."

"No!" Tom stood and slammed his hand to the table. Wheeler jumped at the sound and Mary could see his lower lip trembling.

"We'll not be runnin' or livin' in fear," Tom continued. "Fifteen years we've been diggin' and sweatin' on this land. We've had snakes and cougars, and bears that can rip a horse to shreds. Fifteen years we've been fighting to make our way."

He looked at Jane who silently nodded her approval. She understood her husband had already made his decision and her place was to support that decision whether she agreed or not.

Tom touched the bible on the mantle and seemed to regain the internal peace he so fervently sought from God. Mary watched him caress the leather book and tried to imagine how God could have written the words. It seemed to her that if God was as powerful as people said He was, he'd be able to talk to people in a different way. He wouldn't have to write words in a book. He wouldn't let people die or let wind storms and hail destroy the harvests in men's lives. And she was sure He wouldn't let anyone be killed by Indians. Tom took his seat across from Jeb and again lowered his voice to calm his friend.

"Jeb," he said. "We're thankin' ya for letting us know, but, I don't believe the French or Indians will be makin' it this far."

"But, Tom!" Jeb's voice was frantic. "They're only a few miles from . . ."

Tom placed a hand on Jeb's shoulder. Mary could see the strength filling her father's body. "Now hold on. I heard tell Colonel Washington is gathering his troops plenty fast. My own brother William told us, just before he went off to join the army, that Washington has a load of troops and the French and Indians are scattered everywhere."

He got up and firmly pulled Mary and Jane close to his sides. Mary felt he was like a tree, sheltering her from all she heard. Trees were peaceful, and forever.

"I got me a fine, strong family here," he said. "And a farm my young cousin George would love to steal for his own. No way I'll be leavin' what's mine."

He gave Jane and Mary a loving squeeze and smiled at them to reassure them he was right. Then he rejoined Wheeler at the table, patting his hand to comfort him.

"We're bound to trust in God, Jeb. And in our fighting men. The only smoke we'll be seein' is the Seneca pipe of peace."

Wheeler looked at his hardy friend. Mary could see him searching Tom's eyes, trying to believe what he was saying. He looked at John and Jesse but John shook his head no, only slightly, afraid to disagree with his father. Mary questioned John with her eyes and John whispered to her.

"You can't fight death with a bible."

Mary nodded, but wasn't sure which side she believed. After a moment Wheeler shook his head, the fear and anguish returning to his face.

"Not me, Tom," he said, almost apologizing. "I got my family comin' this way in a wagon. We'll be headin' back East, where it's civilized, just as soon as we can."

Tom looked at him and nodded his head in understanding. He knew his friend didn't have the same faith he did. He knew most of Wheeler's courage had left him as soon as he got off the ship. Wheeler wasn't an Irishman. To Tom, an Irishman had a duty to God and family and would fight to the death to protect it.

"Then, my friend," he said. "You'll be needing a place to stay the night, and a fresh horse to take with you."

He turned to his family, in charge, in control.

"Mary, I want you to go on over to the Thompsons' tonight and get the horse I loaned them."

Jane cautiously interrupted him. "Tom? Through the woods? At night?"

"Well," Tom conceded. "She can leave at daybreak and be back by noon. Got chores and prayers anyway. John. Jesse. I want you to fix up that extra harness and have it ready for Mr. Wheeler."

He turned back to Wheeler, kindly.

"Jeb, you and your family will share our prayers tonight and be on your way tomorrow. The Lord will keep you safe, Lad, don't you be worryin' no more."

✦◈✦ ◈ ✦◈✦

A fine, grey mist settled on the open farmyard the next day. Mary had made her way through the woods to the Thompsons' and had almost forgotten what Jeb Wheeler had said the day before. A few times she felt someone was watching her. Once she thought she heard a voice. The trees reached at her with their still bare branches. The slush of old, dead leaves, softened by the spring thaw, clawed at her feet as she made her way. She tried to think of what her father would do, what he would feel. Her mother would walk straight and proud, but her father, she was sure, would walk with an angry step and a powerful glare. He'd try to frighten away any intruders. She tried to mimic them both, alternating between gruesome looks and proud, detached walking. She laughed at the way she knew she looked. She decided, instead, to say her prayers. She needed the practice and they pushed away her fear.

By the time she walked to the clearing close to her farm, her fear was gone. Her father was never wrong. They were safe. The corn would be high in the fall and the family would be together.

The sun burst through the mist and warmed her face as she pulled the horse behind her into the quiet yard. Suddenly she stopped. The yard was too quiet. Deadly quiet. No axes. No singing. No cries from Matt. Her eyes darted from the house to the barn to the fields. She felt her panic knot in her chest. Pulling the horse as hard as she could she ran into the yard.

"Papa?" Mama?"

The yard was a blur as she raced her eyes across it to the sheep, the horses, back to the woods. She stopped, squeezing her legs together to keep from wetting her dress. Then she heard Tom's faint voice from the barn.

"Mary? That you, lass?"

She let go of the horse and began a full run toward the barn. She was afraid to know what was there, but she knew she had to see, to be near her family even if it meant death. The barn seemed farther than it had ever been before. She was panting, cold from the mist, her eyes blurred with tears. When she got to the door she skidded to a stop. A few feet away was the possibility of death. Her eyes fixed on the door, waiting for death to find her.

But it wasn't death. Tom came out wiping his hands and smiling.

"Mary? That you?"

Mary could feel the life go out of her body. She couldn't move. She could hardly breathe.

"Mary? What happened? What's wrong?"

She stumbled into Tom's arms, clinging and grabbing at his flaxen shirt.

"Papa. Papa. I thought. I . . . I thought . . ."

"Now, now. You thought what, child? Don't be lettin' fear fill your head. A child's life is for livin', not for fearin'."

He gently cupped her chin to look at him. Mary felt he was taller than she remembered. His hair curled from the mist and gave him a more gentle look.

"If there be anyone coming to harm this family they'll not be touching a hair on your beautiful head. I promise you."

"I'm sorry, Papa. I just don't understand."

She held tightly to her father as he thought how to answer her. Touching him, feeling him, even smelling him near her seemed to push her blood back through her veins and wash away her fear.

"Don't know as I really understand myself," Tom said. "We come here to farm and hunt and live, same as them. Could be they're not God-fearin' like we are, so they don't know how to share."

Tom sat her down on a splitting log and pulled another piece of trunk to sit near her.

"I think it's the French been rilin' them. The French want their land. People like us, we're few and far. I don't think the Indians mind us so much."

"But the French are with them?"

"Suppose that's a way to do it. Get the enemy on your side."

Mary thought for a moment as Tom just patiently waited for her to feel better.

"Pa? Do you think they like corn?"

Tom's blue eyes twinkled. "Well, I'm sure I don't know. Are you wantin' to invite them to a corn roast?"

"Yes. I thought that, if they come, and the corn is ready, we could share it and, well, maybe they'd see there's no reason to be fighting."

Tom smiled and hugged her tight. Mary could see the pride in his face.

"Mary, Mary. Your Ma and I are lucky ones, indeed. Now, gather up that horse and get to helpin' your Mama with breakfast."

Tom kissed her on the forehead and patted her on her way. As he went back into the barn Mary could hear him singing the Irish tune that seemed to belong to him. She hummed along as she tied the horse to the rail beside the house.

Just then Wheeler came out, grabbing his gun and taking the reins from Mary. Mary stared at the gun, forcing a smile.

"In case I see turkey on the way back to my place. Gotta get a bag of grain I left there. A man has to feed his family."

He waved and rode away. Andy Wheeler, Jeb's blond, ten year old, son ran out of the house onto the porch. He was waving after his father, but Jeb didn't see him. Mary sensed his anxiety and quietly put an arm around his shoulder. Andy sighed and lowered his head as if he was about to cry.

"Don't worry, Andy. Your Pa'll be back before the core pone's brown."

Inside the farmhouse Jane, Frances Wheeler, her two babies and baby Matt were all gathered around the table. Jane was busily putting her long hair up with a comb. Mary and Andy came in and helped to get ready for breakfast. Mary loved the look of her mother's hair. It was much redder than hers, and longer. She daydreamed of a time when hers would be as long. She would let it hang down her shoulders, maybe to the ground. Her husband would be tall and handsome, with a large farm and enough money to buy her fine combs and ribbons. She'd have a dozen children, half girls, half boys. The girls would be beautiful, and the boys as strong as Tom. Suddenly there was a gunshot. Then two more shots. Frances dropped a plate she was holding, grabbed her two babies close to her and began to cry. Jane quickly took Matt in one arm and the bible in her hand. Mary saw her mother's lips moving in prayer. She wanted to say everything was fine. That Pa was right and there was no danger.

She looked at the closed door, then the gun over the mantle. Through the dried skin covering the window she saw John and Jesse running into the woods.

The door slammed open and echoed off the wall. Mary felt her mother's gasp but couldn't seem to find her own breath. Through the open door she could see Jeb Wheeler's bloodied body lying on the ground. Close to him was the horse from the Thompsons'. Frances Wheeler screamed at the sight of her husband and Mary saw all sanity leave her face.

Beyond the horse was a blue-coated Frenchman binding Tom's hands behind his back. Mary was confused at her father's stance. He wasn't fighting. He wasn't resisting. His face had the faraway look he often had when he missed his mother or thought of Ireland. Yet he seemed as dead as the body near the horse.

Two men dressed in leggings and deer skin, in a way Mary had never seen, were guarding her father. At first it seemed a dream. Then, as suddenly as the shots had been fired, Mary realized that these were the Shawnee Indians and the French.

Two more Shawnee appeared at the door. Jane gasped again and her prayers became louder. A Frenchman ran in and grabbed Frances by the arm. She struggled to hold onto her two babies as the man dragged, then pushed her outside. Mary watched as the Frenchman pushed her by her dead husband, making her trip over Jeb's lifeless hand. She fell to the ground, her babies falling beside her screaming with terror.

Another Shawnee took Mary's arm, and still another frightened her from behind. He was stroking her hair. She, too, was pushed through the door. She tried to fight back, her Irish temper that her father loved seemed like another body beside her. She kicked and pulled away, grabbing her mother's hair brush to use as a club.

"Mary, no!" Jane screamed. "Go peacefully."

Mary stiffened her body with rage and was thrown out the door. A Frenchman ripped the bible from Jane's hand, examined it for a moment, then threw it to the floor. From outside Mary could see her mother reaching for the book, crying, almost calling it toward her like a wounded child.

The captors were all over the house throwing things against the walls, crushing chairs, tossing plates. Whenever they found a stash of food they would quickly stuff it into pouches they wore at their sides. The Frenchmen seemed in control. They treated the Shawnee like students, teaching them the proper way to destroy.

Tom was lined up with the others, but he was silent. Mary saw a distance in his eyes she had never seen before. She looked to him for help but he didn't look back. In one short moment of terror his dreams and his strength had vanished.

"Be brave, Mary," Jane whispered. "Trust God. Stand up straight and tall."

Mary automatically obeyed. Andy squeezed Frances' hand, but Frances made no effort to respond. He then took Mary's hand, wiping his tears on his sleeve. The captives could only stand and watch as destruction ripped through their lives.

Once or twice Mary tried to look at Jeb Wheeler. She prayed he was really alive and would jump up at just the right moment and free them. She could see Tom's hands bound behind him. She wondered why he wasn't trying to get untied, to save his family as he always said he would.

The captors surrounded them. Shawnee and Frenchmen touched them, examined them, felt their hair, their arms. Frances Wheeler stood motionless. One of the Frenchman pinched her arm. Then he slapped her face, but she didn't respond. Her two babies cried in her arms without comfort.

A Shawnee came close to Mary and touched her. His eyes seemed almost friendly to Mary as he stroked and petted her hair. She turned her head away, back and forth, to avoid his touch. Then he turned to Jane and touched her hair. Mary saw her mother's body slump for the first time.

"Rouge . . . red," a Frenchman said. The Shawnee he spoke to nodded understanding.

"You'll bring a good bounty," he said to Jane. "Both of you."

He motioned to Mary and touched her face.

"A beauty you are."

Mary looked at Tom, her eyes pleading for his help. Jane hushed her before she could speak.

"Your Pa's in no shape for talking. Save your strength. Trust in the Lord. Do as your Pa always told us and trust in the Lord."

Mary couldn't help searching her father's eyes for some sign of fight, but Tom stayed silent, his body limp and defeated.

The captives were lined up with Tom in front. A Shawnee pulled at Tom's shirt to force him to walk. The others were pushed and prodded by their captors until they were trotting toward the woods.

As they passed the newly planted corn field Mary slowed and bent to touch the earth. She wished the corn had been ready. She wished she could see its tassels blowing in the breeze. A Shawnee whipped her from behind, prodding her to trot with the others. No one had ever struck her before. She tried to look at the Indian's face, to make him stop, to make him see she was a young girl and he should stop. But he whipped her again and she knew any fight was useless. She crushed the dirt in her hand and spun to throw it at her captor. Again she was whipped and the lash jerked her forward. She managed one more glance toward the woods, searching quickly for any sign of John or Jesse. She was sure they were safe and would find a way to rescue them. She was sure. But she silently prayed.

2

John and Jesse were tired and cold. It seemed they had run miles, the chill of spring and the coldness of death pushed them to exhaustion. They looked back, afraid, then stopped and searched the road ahead. A horse was approaching.

"It's not running. Not even trotting," John said to Jesse.

They quickly took cover behind budding bushes and awaited a view of the rider. Jesse whimpered and his body twitched like the tail of a cat frightened by a predator. John put his arm around him and covered his mouth with his hand.

The horse came closer. The boys watched the road. John thought he could hear someone humming. As the humming got louder John took his hand off Jesse's mouth.

"Only one other person knows that song," He said. "Cousin George learned that song from Pa."

Jesse started to run out of the bushes toward the horse, but John quickly grabbed his arm.

"Wait. We have to be sure. I almost wish it was anyone but George."

"If it is cousin George he'll help." Jesse's voice was shaking as he spoke. John put a hand on his shoulder to comfort him.

"Just take it slow, Jess. Much as I hate him, if it's George, I'll ask for his help."

George Jemison rode into view. He was a sloppy man not much older than John's eighteen. As he came closer John wondered if the horse he rode was really his or just another anything begged or stolen from someone who trusted his Irish blue eyes.

Jesse focused on the rider and could no longer hold himself back.

"Cousin George! Cousin George!"

George pulled his horse to a frightened stop. He shaded his eyes, but he didn't grab his gun or act afraid.

"Who ya be? State your business," he said.

Jesse ran from the bushes, stumbling in his urgency and exhaustion. John walked out defiantly, soberly.

"Ah, it's the Jemison boys. Come to greet me did ya?"

John coolly grabbed the horse's reins as Jesse shuddered in tears beside him.

"We just need some help."

"Oh? Not money, I hope."

Jesse interrupted the frigid standoff.

"It's the Indians! And the French! They got the family."

Jesse could no longer hold back his tears. John's gaze remained fixed on George.

"Indians?" Said George. "When? You mean Shawnee?"

"'Bout an hour ago," John said. You willin' to help or not?"

Jesse grabbed George's leg. "They killed them all. We coulda helped, but we ran. We coulda helped."

George dismounted, brushing nonexistent dust from his black woolen clothes.

"Now hold on. How you know it was Indians? Did ya see 'em?"

Both boys nodded.

"A bunch of them, or a small group?"

"Four or five," said John. "With just as many French."

"Burn the place, did they?"

Jesse wiped back his tears.

"Don't know. We saw them comin', and we ran. We coulda helped. Pa never knew . . ."

George interrupted. "Aye. Don't sound like a killin' party.

27

I hear tell there's been plenty of captives taken lately. They're selling them at the forts for labor. Get a good price, too!"

George checked the trinkets and junk tied to his horse and remounted. He was slow and methodical. John's impatience showed in his glare. He eyed George's gun, but George quickly snugged it closer to him, proving it was his.

"You two stay here. Get behind something and stay here. I'll get my friend, Mr. Gates. Don't worry. The Shawnee won't be hurtin' the family. They got a custom of giving whites to each other in exchange for one of theirs that's been killed. Your family's either gonna live with them or be traded by them. They get a good price. A damn good price!"

He turned and trotted his horse back the way he came. John stared as he disappeared and kicked the ground angry and frustrated. Jesse's sobbing broke his mood and he put his arm around his brother to lead him toward some trees.

"Calm down, Jess. I sure ain't happy about George helpin', but I've heard some of Mr. Gates. He's some kind of expert or something. I heard he can track an Indian the same as a bear and he's been further west than most men can dream. Fact is, I even heard he might be part Cherokee. Come on, Jess. You don't want Mama to know you've been crying, do ya? We'll find them. Pa won't let nothin' bad happen."

The woods turned to thick forest as the captives kept up their run. Finally the whipping stopped as they came to a small grassy clearing. They were ordered into a circle and pushed to the still frozen ground. Mary's tears were almost ice on her cheeks, but she didn't make a sound. Andy moaned and sobbed his way to the ground as a Frenchman kicked dirt at him in disgust.

Mary looked at Frances. Her babies had not stopped crying and, though she cuddled them close to her, her face was like a dead deer, eyes staring at nothing, the gaze fixed and lifeless.

Mary leaned toward her mother, but Jane offered no

physical comfort. Instead she reached out to her captors, grabbing at their pants, their hands.

"Please," she pleaded. "Please. Some water for my family? For our friends?"

Mary had never seen her mother so torn, so ragged. Her body was crusted with dirt, her hair tangled and dry. She wanted to help. She felt like she should hold her mother, rock her, comfort her somehow.

She looked at her Pa, still lifeless and spent. Her body and heart cried out to him, this man she adored and respected. He was her man of the woods. Strong. Resilient. He always had an answer, a comforting word. He was kind and God-fearing.

She stared at him and tried to remember any time he hadn't responded to her. Tried to remember only yesterday, only that morning, when his eyes twinkled and his stance was proud.

Once he had failed her. Only once. When his mother died he drank a bottle of rum and changed. She remembered going to him in the night, needing the strength of his words to soothe her sorrow. But the smell of rum mixed with his own and his eyes were angry. He was angry with God and everyone in the world who wasn't Him. He couldn't listen. He couldn't hold her. She remembered how glad she was when morning came and he was real again. Only once had he failed her. And now.

"Please? Some food? Just a little?"

The captors ignored Jane's pleading. She started to rise to get their attention.

"Some water? We're so tired. For the children?"

A Frenchman finally turned to her, his gaze intent and degrading, stripping her even more of any pride.

"Water? You crave water?"

"Yes." Jane seemed almost relieved. "Yes. For my daughter. The young boy."

The man travelled her body with his eyes.

"Your bodies make water. Drink the water from your bodies."

He laughed and walked away to join the others. Defeated,

Jane slumped to the ground. Mary moved closer to her untouched, unnoticed.

"Mama, what will happen? If they mean to kill us, why must we thirst for it?"

"My child, I'm not knowin' the future. But we must be strong. We must hold on. Hold onto our faith."

"Hold onto our faith," Mary repeated. "Have to hold onto our faith."

She wasn't sure what that meant. Was God here now? Was He running and tired and cold and thirsty? She tried to believe, tried to remember the hours she'd spent with her mother learning about the beginning of life and sinning and commandments from a man she'd never met. She thought God was more something inside of every person, a part of them they had to reach for. Once she had asked her mother if God was a real person or just something in the air. Jane had slapped her face. Not hard. Not with any kind of hate. Just hard enough to make Mary know she should never question again.

They huddled together with lifeless touches and, though fighting it, fell asleep.

※━━━※

It rained in the morning. It was the cold, chilling rain that seemed to seep into your bones and make them cold from the inside out. The captors hustled the group to their feet and prodded them into a run again. Mary felt the bitterness, and her body ached from her frozen sleep. The rain splashed at her face and arms, whipping her as hard as the man who followed her. She stuck out her tongue to catch the rain. Andy saw her and copied. Soon all but the babies and Tom were catching the rain with their tongues, licking it from their arms, their hands, even their clothes.

Buckskin shoes and boots stumbled and stuck in the mud. The smell of the rain and mud made Mary think of the corn field. The rain was good for the corn. She wondered if she'd ever see a field of corn again. She thought of corn pone and corn bread. Her empty stomach signalled her other senses so she could smell and taste corn. It almost took away her hunger. Almost.

As the dawn turned to midday the rain turned to snow. A heavy, wet snow that stuck to Mary's cheeks and felt like a blanket too heavy to move in her fatigue.

"We must be heading toward the mountains," Jane said.

The mountains. Mary had never seen them. Their farm was in a valley surrounded by trees and grass high enough to hide a horse. Mountains were something majestic and close to Heaven. Mountains were something you couldn't climb unless you were very strong or very special. Her Papa had told her they were God's hills. She tripped through the wet sloppiness beneath her and looked from side to side. She couldn't tell if they were running up or down.

The snow was thicker now, the flakes like giant tufts of fur. Now and then a family of fir trees would block the biting wind and the wetness and Mary eyed them thankfully. The group slipped and slid, struggling to maintain the grueling pace set by their captors. One of the babies screamed as Frances slipped to the ground. Mary quickly took the baby in her arms, chiding herself for not helping Mrs. Wheeler before. She felt better now. Almost stronger. It scared her to think she might be growing used to her predicament. The running was easier. She realized they were now running downhill, out of the mountains.

The snow abruptly stopped, melting quickly into the warmer ground. A light dusting remained as the group was once again huddled in a circle. Their clothes were wet and torn. Bloody scratches mixed with cold wetness. They huddled closer trying desperately to stay warm.

The captors took food stolen from the farm house and passed it out among the captives. Mary watched the now stale corn pone fall and crumble to the ground. No one moved. No one's hunger was powerful enough to overcome his despair.

31

Slowly Jane gathered the pieces.

"The food is from God," she said. "We must eat. Children, eat. You'll need your strength."

Mary broke a piece of the pone and moved closer to Tom. She put a piece close to his lips, urging him to taste. Tom glanced at her as a stranger and turned away.

"Papa, please. It's not your fault. You didn't know. Please eat, Papa."

Mary bit into the pone and chewed with exaggeration. Her salty tears flavored the pieces as she watched Tom's silence. She rubbed his arm, leaned her head on his shoulder, desperately but affectionately touching him, as someone trying to wake the dead.

"Oh, Papa. We need you. Remember the farm? Remember how you said we shouldn't live in fear? Hear me, Papa! Hear me!"

She patted and petted his head, humming his tune through stifled sobs. Jane tended to Matt as well as she could. Mary wondered why her mother didn't try to rouse Tom. She seemed apart from him, distanced in anger and grief, as if he had been dead for some time and she had not yet faced all the reality of that death.

Mary watched her father sink further into despair. She wrapped an arm around him, trying to warm him.

"Don't be afraid, Papa. Don't be afraid."

A tear escaped Tom's eye forging a path through the crusted mud on his face.

"Don't worry, Papa. No one sees. No one knows. I love you. I'll always love you. You'll always be my Papa. I'll love you forever."

She lay her head on his shoulder and ate the pone. A Shawnee approached and quietly began unlacing her shoe.

"Mary, don't move," Jane commanded.

Mary instinctively tried to pull away, but the glare of the Indian stopped her. He pulled off one shoe, then the other. Gently and with purpose he removed her stockings.

"Oh, Mama! What does it mean?"

The Shawnee pulled a pair of moccasins from his pouch and carefully put them on Mary's feet. They were plain, soft, warm. Satisfied, he nodded and looked at Andy. Another Shawnee had done the same to him. He stood alone, shaking, crying, looking in all directions, unsure.

"Mary, I believe you'll be leaving us soon. Your life will be spared. Remember your name. Practice your prayers. And your English. Do not forget your English. Don't run. For sure you'll be killed if you try."

Mary didn't understand. Her mother was calm, dignified, sending her on her way. But where? And why?

"Trust in God," Jane said. "He will bless you, my daughter."

Her mother's hand reached out to her crushing any last hope in her fingers.

"Be good, Mary. Be strong . . ."

A Shawnee pulled Mary away while another dragged a crying Andy deeper into the forest. Mary tried to fight, tried to hold onto her mother's hand. Jane seemed to let go, to let her daughter be taken. The Indian was strong, but not punishing. Mary couldn't hold back her sobs. It never occurred to her that she would have to face this awful thing alone.

"Don't cry, Mary. We're with you, my daughter. We're always with you. God is with you. Don't cry."

Mary screamed. "Mama! Papa? Do something! I love you! Please don't let them take me. I love you!"

Soon she could no longer see her family or anyone except Andy and their Shawnee companion. Andy sobbed next to her. She hugged him close to her and tried to hum Tom's Irish tune to quiet him. She was afraid his crying would mean death to them both. The Shawnee motioned for them to lie down for the night. The Indian laid down, too. Andy quieted, but didn't stop. Mary sang to him.

"All the young lassies, and all the young lads. Rise up in the morning to greet the new day. The Lord is a watchin' and lending a hand. To the lassies, and laddies who care for His land."

Singing her father's song quieted young Andy and, soon, Mary heard his rhythmic breathing of sleep. The man also slept, but his rhythm seemed different to Mary. It was slower, almost breezy. She looked at his face in the dim light. It was tighter than hers. Stronger. Except for his hair, which was dark and short, and tied back to avoid entanglement with forest brush, he didn't seem much different from any other man.

Andy shivered in her arms. She drew his body closer and cradled his head in her arm. The aching and coldness in her body seemed to numb as she strained to hear any sounds from her family, but the forest was silent.

At dawn the snow fell again. Mary and Andy were awakened and brought to their feet. All the Shawnee and French were with them, and more had joined them sometime in the night. They prodded and whipped, trying to get them to run. Mary looked back for her family. The whip hurt. It was strange how she hadn't really felt it before. She had welts and fresh bruises, but she hadn't really felt them until now.

A Frenchman grabbed her arms and spun her to the ground. He kicked at her feet as if she was a dog who stubbornly refused to move. She got up from the cold earth, but still resisted. Her family was behind her somewhere. Whatever their fate, she needed to be with them. Again she was whipped from behind. Andy started crying, pulling her with him. Mary looked at his pleading face, then back at the forest behind her. She remembered her mother's words. If she ran she'd be killed. She must be good, and not cry. Her mother was with her. A Frenchman prodded her back with the butt of his gun. She obeyed.

The snow stopped sometime in the afternoon. Mary and Andy sat together with their captors forming a circle around a small fire. Everyone seemed busy with a task. Some fashioned weapons, others guarded. The Indian who watched over them the night before dragged a deer carcass into the strange camp. He motioned to Mary, but Mary didn't know what he wanted. He pushed her closer to the carcass and motioned again. She looked at the dead animal's eyes. She thought of Frances and the babies. Disgusted and distraught she turned away. The Shawnee pushed her to the ground, then held her still so she could watch him. He pulled out his tomahawk and began chopping up the carcass, tossing pieces of it in a boiling pot. Ears, eyes, the tail. It seemed that everything was thrown into the pot. When he was finished he dragged her closer to the fire. He took water from his pouch and added it to the deer parts. Then he stirred the concoction, motioning to Mary to copy. She tried to turn away, but he forced her back and handed her the crude wooden spoon. Reluctantly she stirred.

How different this was from the cooking at home. Her father and brothers always cleaned and carved the game they killed. She remembered her mother saying she couldn't stand the sight of blood, and would keep her distance from any animal carcass until it was properly cleaned for cooking. Then, only the choicest parts were stewed in a kettle with potatoes or corn. Never any part of the head or tail. Never any part that wasn't the best.

She watched Andy being silently instructed in the making of a tomahawk. Two Indians on either side of him wrapped pieces of deer hide around a sharpened stone to secure it to a shaft. They tried to get Andy to copy. She hoped Andy would seize a tomahawk and strike. She hoped he wouldn't. She knew he couldn't.

One Shawnee pulled a tomahawk from his belt and raised it above Andy's head. Andy jumped back, afraid. He started crying, disgusting the Indian. The Indians pulled the tomahawk material away and left Andy sitting by himself. Mary could see he was trying intensely to rally his courage, but he

35

was young and his father's son. She knew he could try to be brave. She knew also that any courage he found would be superficial and insignificant.

The stewed deer parts were placed in eager waiting hands. Mary and Andy tried to eat, but the cooking of the deer had made Mary nauseous, and Andy didn't seem interested.

When their captors had finished eating, they got right back to work. A Shawnee across the fire from Mary pulled open a large pouch. From it he slowly removed a bloodied piece of hair. Mary instantly gagged on the thick saliva in her mouth. A Frenchman instructed him in the cleaning of the scalp. He scraped the skin and blood away, then stretched it across a hoop, holding it near the fire to dry. Mary felt Andy's fingers digging into her skin as he buried his face in her shoulder. The Frenchman seemed pleased with the Indian's work.

The Shawnee pulled out another. And another. The next one was her mother's long red hair.

"That's my Mama . . . my Mama!"

Without thinking she pushed Andy aside and tried to run. Right into the arms of a Frenchman.

"They would not have been killed if we were not pursued," he said.

Mary struggled to pull away, kicking and punching at him with her all her might. They had killed her mother, butchered her, and then dared to steal her hair. The man grabbed her hard, forcing her to look at him.

"We will be pursued no more."

Mary froze. She felt the last drops of hope trickle from her body forming a pool at her feet. The man let go and she slumped to the ground. Visions of her mother's dancing hair, her father's twinkling eyes played before her. She couldn't look at the fire. She could smell singed hair and flesh. She pulled the moccasins from her feet and flung them into the trees. The Frenchman came back to her, stuffing the scalps into a bloodied pouch.

"They bring a good price. Your mother's was the finest of all."

She stared at the pouch as he walked away. A part of her wanted to reach for it, to save whatever part of her family she could. The smoke from the fire burned her eyes. The smell grabbed at her stomach. She heaved and retched into the mud around her.

John, Jesse, George and Gates walked single file into the spring foliage, searching for any signs of a trail. George was last, and not as diligent as the others. He seemed almost calm and distracted.

"So, John, lad. Had your father improved on the farm any, before this unsavory incident?"

John kept walking, ignoring him, preoccupied with his search.

"Had he gotten more seed in? Cleared more fields?"

George waited for an answer.

"Fine man, your Pa. A good, hard working lad. Do ya think he'll be back on the farm when this is over? Or do ya think he'll go back . . . ?"

John spun around and raised his borrowed gun to George.

"What difference does it make to you? All you be wantin' is his land, is that it? Is it?"

He cocked his gun, ready to shoot. Jesse grabbed his arm, but John pulled away, still aiming and ready.

"John, what are you doing? This here is family, like it or not. He's our cousin, John."

George seemed relieved. "Yes! Listen to him, Lad. I'm family. White, like you."

Gates, a lean, quiet man, squatted near a tree to wait out the confrontation.

"You're family 'cause you bear the Jemison name," John said. "But you never treated my Pa like you was family. Always

37

beggin' for money, jealous of his land. And bein' white makes no difference anymore. I'd sooner shoot you now than ever let you set a foot on my Pa's farm. It's as sure as winter you'll never cheat our family again."

He lowered the gun, spitting on the ground, and left Jesse looking at George. Gates silently joined him and gave him a thoughtful glance.

"The devil with him," said John.

Gates answered. "It would seem he knows the Devil already."

They continued walking and searching.

"I don't even know what I'm looking for," said John. "I haven't seen one twig cracked, one blade of grass turned down."

"Uh-hmmm," answered Gates. "It's the Indian way. They leave one man behind to bring the grass up straight. . .so's you can't follow them. Trick is to keep your nose up in the air."

John looked at him, confused. He stuck his nose up, sniffing the air, checking Gates to see how he did it.

"You mean you can smell 'em," John asked?

"Them? No. Indian's like any other man. You smell for smoke. That'll lead us to them."

John sniffed again. "Do you smell smoke?"

"Nope, not yet. But this is the general direction of Fort Pitt. Most of the captives are taken there."

Gates paused and gave John another glance.

"By the way, boy. If we do smell smoke, you'd best hope we also smell deer or turkey."

John was puzzled, but he listened to the stranger.

"If we're heading toward this Fort Pitt, shouldn't we be near the river?"

"You're thinkin', boy," Gates said. "But the river's too shallow here. They can't go up river for a ways yet."

When Mary and Andy reached the river with their captors they were loaded into a canoe hidden in the brush. Their torn clothes made them feel almost naked. Mary was seated near the front, the pouch with the scalps placed beside her. Two canoes followed as they headed up river.

Andy sat behind Mary and lightly kicked at her back to get her attention. Mary turned slightly, unnoticed, but afraid to be obvious. Andy jerked his head toward the side of the canoe.

"What do you mean?" Mary whispered.

"Now's our chance. We can jump and swim down river," Andy said. "Bound to reach some friendly folk."

"Bound to drown . . . or be killed, you mean."

Mary felt Andy's frustration, but she didn't trust an escape. They had no direction, no knowledge of their surroundings.

"Rather be drowned than scalped!" Andy held fast to the side of the swift canoe. Mary caught herself, ready to sob. She took a breath, looked at the pouch next to her and grimaced.

"I won't be goin' against my mother's words." She turned away from Andy, her words final. "I won't run. 'Specially when I don't know where I'd be runnin'."

Though she'd never seen a fort before, Mary was sure the structure up ahead was just that. It was an eerie place, looking out on the river like a stone soldier.

"That's Fort Pitt," Andy said.

"I know," Mary whispered. "My Pa told me about it. A big one. Three turrets. The river forks on both sides."

"Maybe we'll be saved after all," Andy said. "Yep, that's Fort Pitt. Full of scoundrels, thieves and Indians, my Pa said. But there must be someone there could recognize us as white."

The Shawnees pulled the canoe to shore and ordered the children out. Mary went to one side, Andy the other. A Frenchman held Andy still as another scrubbed his face and combed his hair. The same was done to Mary. Then a Shawnee mixed some herbs and berries in a mortar bowl. Taking a smooth stick, he painted their hair and faces a bright red. Satisfied, they proudly led the children into the fort.

It was a large, busy open place. There were French, Seneca and a few whites crossing paths, all seemingly on some mission, all oblivious to the entrance of the captives. The children were led to an empty wooden stockade and thrown to the dirt floor. The door slammed shut behind them, closing them in darkness.

Small patches of smoke dotted the early sky as the search party closed slowly on the muddy clearing. John and Gates led the way, but John stopped, choking on the smell, the stench of death.

"That there is the fires of Hell, Boy," said Gates to John. "Burning flesh. Can haunt your senses forever."

John continued coughing, choking, putting his coat in front of his face to block the stench. He suddenly realized what Gates was saying. Quickly his eyes darted through the debris of the fires. He saw glimpses of body parts, ashes. Y-shaped stands were spread between smoldering fires. Charred hands, only hands, hung off one side but folded together as if still praying. One stand looked like it held a baby's body, wrinkled and blackened, its bones falling in pieces to the ground.

Tears welled in John's eyes, a scream building inside him. "My Ma? And Pa? God, no! Oh, God no!"

He went to his knees and covered his face in anguish. Jesse froze with fear some distance away as Gates carefully searched the debris.

"Recognize any of these?" Gates asked, showing John some charred clothing and a woman's hair comb.

John got to his feet, afraid to look, and afraid not to. He grabbed the comb from Gates, petting it, smelling it. Cradling the comb in his arms, he walked away softly crying.

Gates shook his head in sympathy, then, to anyone listening, he said, "It's the Indian way. It's their religion."

He looked toward the fires and took off his brimmed hat.

"It's their way of pleasin' their Creator, avenging those Indians who died. It's the way of the Iroquois, the Six Nations who live and travel in these parts. The Shawnee ain't part of the Indian Confederacy, but they follow their ways."

George, who had stayed safely away from the discovery, came running to the front, seemingly unbothered by the smoke or smell.

"Is it . . . are they all? Is there any way we can tell if they're all . . . ?"

Gates helped his stumbling. "Don't know. Hard tellin', seein' as they do it this way. Judging by the number of stakes, parts, things like that, I'd say they got eight, maybe more. Can't tell for sure."

George turned to Jesse, still dazed by the sight before him.

"Jesse! How many you say were at your home?"

Jesse didn't answer. George raced to him and tried to shake him from his stupor.

"How many, Lad? How many?"

Jesse tried to count, crying and wiping his nose while he thought.

"I don't know. I'm not sure. Ma, Pa, Mary, Matt, Mrs. Wheeler, the babies, and Andy."

Gates shook his head in sorrow while George recounted on his fingers.

"That be eight, maybe nine if the babies were little. God rest 'em. They got 'em all."

George took off his black hat and placed it on his chest for a moment. Then, using his hat to cover his face, he ran toward the fires.

"We best gather what we can and be gone," he said. "No sense lookin' no further."

John gripped his gun and pointed it at George.

41

"Leave it!"

George stopped cold. "John, what's wrong with you, Lad? You have to save what's yours. For remembrance."

"For tradin', you mean."

"Now, John."

"Leave it, I say. That that burned with 'em, stays with 'em. It's the only burial they'll have and I mean to send them on their way with what's theirs."

Frustrated, but aware that John's aim was straight, George again dusted invisible dirt from his clothes and retreated to pick up his rifle.

"Leave that, too."

"My gun? I can't leave my gun!"

"My Pa gave you that gun. It stays."

George looked at Gates for help.

"I'll walk you back to where we started, George. You won't need the gun."

He walked to John calmly and lowered John's gun.

"Where will you be headed?"

John looked at the comb still nestled in his hand.

"Don't know. Maybe back home."

"Can't go back," Gates said. "Probably burned you out by now."

John looked at him sadly, confused and seemingly alone.

"You gotta understand, Son," said Gates. "They was here first. This is their land and everybody wants it. They're mostly peaceful. Ain't nothin' Indian men like better than lying in the sun, eatin' their catch, their harvest. They most likely been here more than a hundred years before us. A few settlers here and there, they didn't mind. But then we start choppin' down their trees. Killing their deer and elk. Then the French come along and want the land. The best land. Takin' it right out from under the Indians. Next thing you know, those French are bribin' them."

Gates spat on the ground and shook his head.

". . . Giving them trinkets, weapons, killing some along the way, too. Pretty soon, it's a war. Got Seneca around here joinin' with the French 'cause the English treat 'em meaner. The Seneca are the fiercest of the nations. The keepers of the Western door. Ain't nothin' west of the O-hi-o but wilderness, but the Seneca has to guard that door just the same. Just in case."

John looked at the fires, trying to understand.

"But burnin' and killin'. . . like this."

"In their eyes this ain't no different than what we've been doing to them. An eye for an eye, a life for a life. To them, every tree, every bird, every deer is family. We done our share of choppin' and burnin' and killing. The Indians let you and your family alone, until too many started ruining everything. Right or wrong, it's the Indian way. You gotta respect it."

John nodded to Gates. He was sure his Pa would have said the same. He went to Jesse, hugged him, and kept an arm around him to lead him away.

"Guess we'll head on South, see if we can find Grandpa," he said. "Or maybe join up with Washington."

He looked again at the fires.

"No buryin' to be done here. Pa would want his ashes mixin' with the wind. No use bein' where we shouldn't be. We thank ya, Mr. Gates, for all your help."

John and Jesse walked past George without a glance. George tried a wave, but he knew they weren't looking. Gates looked at the fires, put his hat back on, spat again, and left with George trailing behind him.

3

"Papa? That you, Papa?"

The stockade was dark and damp as the door opened. The bright light from outside blinded Mary as she awakened to two male figures standing in the doorway. The Frenchmen entered and dragged a half-asleep Andy by the arm. He tried to wave, to call out to Mary, but he was gone. Mary was alone. She could see light through the closed door, an occasional shadow, but she was alone.

She tried to take comfort in the darkness around her. She felt the ground she sat on, felt its coolness. She sifted the dirt through her fingers. The dried red paint itched her scalp. She wanted to bury her face in the dirt and scrape the paint from her body, but she was afraid.

She remembered her mother and father, and practiced her prayers. "Our Father, who be in Heaven. Tom, Jane, John, Jesse, Matt."

The door opened again. Two women entered and approached Mary, followed by one of the Shawnee captors. He stood proudly over Mary, his arms crossed in front of him, as the Seneca women examined her. They felt her arms, testing the muscle. Mary was proud of her strength, but she recoiled at their touch. They stroked her hair. One of the women spat in her hand and used it to wash away paint from strands of Mary's hair. The red-gold glimmered in the light and the women squealed with enjoyment. One woman motioned to Mary to stand. When she hesitated her captor pulled her to her feet and then resumed his proud stance. The women checked her calf muscles, her teeth, as a buyer checking a horse. They seemed pleased with her appearance. The captor put his hand out just above Mary's head to indicate her shortness. The women shook their heads. It didn't matter. The captor nodded and gave Mary a slight push toward the women. The women stood on either side of Mary, smiling, and the captor left.

"Dehewamus," said the first woman. "De-he-wa-mus."

She poked Mary's chest firmly with each syllable.

"Dehewamus. Two Falling Voices. Your name."

She took the other woman's hand and drew her closer.

"My sister. Now you are also our sister."

Mary looked at one, then the other. She was a gift to them from her captors. They wanted her to be a sister. She eyed the open door, but they saw her look at it.

"No!" The second sister spread her arms to block Mary's path. Mary jumped, cowered, like a trapped animal. The second sister looked at her sternly. "Now you are ours. To replace our fallen brother. Our Shawnee brother has given you to us in friendship."

"You will live with us. Be one with us," said the first sister.

"We are your family," the second sister said.

They gently started removing her clothing. Very slowly each sister took turns pulling off a ragged garment. Each time they'd turn her, examine her. Mary was frightened and embarrassed.

The second sister continued. "Our brother fell in battle, a great warrior. Twenty suns have passed since we sent him on the path of a good Indian. We have waited. Now you are brought to us."

They continued removing her clothing. The first sister motioned to the other and the second sister left. Mary longed to follow her through the open door. She studied the first sister who seemed to have no name. She looked kinder than the other, but more driven, more resolute in her ways. Her eyes were dark and her shiny black hair draped across her back.

The second sister returned with water and rags and a fresh suit of Seneca clothes. They gently bathed her still examining her as they spoke.

"We will leave and travel the O-hi-o, the beautiful river," said the first. "To our village. We will teach you the Seneca ways."

Mary didn't want to learn the Seneca ways. She wanted to be with her family, on the farm, with the corn. Her body shook with humiliation, grief, exhaustion. Tears formed red rivers on her cheeks. The second sister used her hand and gently brushed away the tears.

"Do not be afraid," she said. "A Seneca woman shows no fear. Her tears are her own, to water her soul. You were saved because of your courage. You must always be brave."

Mary felt as if her mother was speaking to her through this strange new sister. She stood erect, composed. She knew her time would come. Someone would find her. Someone would let her go back. For now, she'd wait. She needed shelter and food. The sisters would provide that.

When she emerged from the stockade she looked every bit a Seneca woman, except for her red-gold hair and the whiteness of her face. Even her blue eyes seemed darkened by her days of flight.

Her dress was like a shirt, hanging midway down her hips. Underneath it she wore a gown of skin tied at various places with deer hide. Her leggings were thick and extended into her moccasins. A Seneca petticoat hung lower than the gown and dropped to a few inches above the moccasins. She was dressed for warmth, convenience, necessity, and tradition.

She was led from the fort without a glimpse from anyone there. At the river, the sisters seated her carefully in the center of their canoe and then joined her, one in front, one behind. Another canoe with a few warriors led them down the river.

Mary watched the banks on either side of her, straining to see anyone, anything that might save her. She felt the clothing around her. It was the warmest she'd been since her capture. She touched the cloth, smelled it. Though it was clean and warm, to her it smelled of Indians.

Suddenly she grabbed both sides of the canoe. On the bank to her left was a large clearing with smoky fires every few feet. Parts of bodies hung from poles, some still flaming over ashes. Mary tried to block her face from the stench, the smoke burned her. She looked at the sisters who neither looked toward the banks nor reacted to the smoke. She tried to bury her head in her lap, tried to cover every part of her, to hide herself from the ugly truth that surrounded her. The first sister jabbed her in the back with her paddle to make her sit up and take notice. The sister didn't look at her, just jabbed and went back to paddling.

They paddled for miles through the choppy water. Mary had no sense of direction, no feeling of the way to her home. Aloneness and fear tapped at her mind and she blinked back her urge to scream.

"I wish to relieve myself," she said.

The first sister jabbed her again. "No English!"

The second sister laid down her paddle and raised her dress. She pulled Mary to the opposite side of the canoe to balance the weight. The sister squatted and balanced.

"You may give back to the Earth as I do," she said.

Mary was disgusted, but the bloat in her belly was painful and urgent. The sisters were now her teachers. She would learn from them and wait.

4

Mary arrived at Wiishto, the village her new sisters called home, and was greeted by women of all ages with open arms and friendliness. Her sisters explained that all who were accepted as family were treated with love and kindness. Often her sisters spoke to her in Seneca, and urged her to learn their language so she could be a true Indian, but Mary resisted. Though she learned the Seneca language well and pleased her sisters, she practiced her English whenever she was alone, as her mother had told her. With time, she had her sisters learning as many English words as she in Seneca.

She was immediately taken to a home made of bark and shared it with her sisters and an elder they called Mother. They were kind to her and, though each night she cried for the loss of her true family, time and familiarity made her almost comfortable. She felt she cared for them as she would her family and found herself touching, talking, even, at times, laughing with them as though she was home.

They showed her how to sit on the ground comfortably and made her sit still for hours at a time. They wanted her to be a friend to the earth. She sat on the ground for all meals. She slept on the ground. When a log or a rock was convenient for sitting it was shunned in favor of the ground.

At first Mary's body didn't seem to conform, but eventually she found it easy to sit with her legs crossed and do almost any chore given to her.

She mostly watched other women's children. Her sisters thought she needed much more practice in cooking and cleaning deer and elk. Once, when one of the children struck another, Mary shouted that he should stop and firmly placed him on the ground away from the others. The first sister came to her quickly.

"Dehewamus," she said. "You must learn faster the way of the Seneca. No voice is raised against a Seneca child. Our children learn justice and honesty, not rage and anger. If one seems ready to strike at another you must find the reason. Then you must help the child find the reason, discover what evil may be hiding in him, so that the two of you, together, can overcome that evil."

Mary was surprised that the good behavior of the children came from fairness and not cruelty. Yet they also seemed disciplined. The next time a child seemed to strike against another she tried her sister's suggestion and calmly seated the two beside her to ask them why there was trouble between them.

"The fly of the deer was on his back, ready to bite, so I struck it and killed it," the first child said.

The other child was surprised. "Why didn't you tell me of the fly? I thought you struck me out of hate, so I readied to strike you back."

The two children laughed and returned to their play. They learned to speak to each other first, before striking, and Mary also learned.

Each day was the same as the last. The routine of the Seneca was much different from the days Mary remembered. White people, her people, seemed to fill their time with more variety, each day a new adventure or crisis. The Seneca days were mellow and easy. Each knew his job. Each job, because it was shared by others, seemed easy and almost peaceful. There was no jealousy. No petty quarrels. Mary thought of all the times she had fought with John or Jesse over the best ear of corn or the unwillingness of any of them to clean up after the horses. This was truly a different life, a different world. At times Mary thought it might be God's world.

Even the animals ran free and were taken care of by the house that harbored them last. Mary thought that would please God as her father had often told her God loved all creatures.

When she thought of her father she could also see the large oak door of their cabin. She remembered her father telling her it was to keep away evil, be they people or beast. In her house of bark there were two doors, one at each end, but they weren't oak or wood. The doors were there to vary the draft through the house so the fires would continually burn and the direction of the smoke could be controlled. Visitors were never treated as outsiders, but were, instead, accepted as family in the house. Mary often saw strangers enter, take food by the fire, sleep the night, and leave without a word. Her Seneca family only nodded to them in friendliness, and made sure the pots of food were always full and the skins for sleeping were warm and plentiful. Each day Mary said what prayers she could remember, but each day she grew closer to her Seneca sisters and brothers and felt more content to be with them.

PART II

5

The cornfields were high. The small Seneca village nestled near the Ohio was full of frolic and merriment in the Festival of Fall. The long war was over and the Seneca could go back to peace. Long bark houses with puffs of smoke seeping through the roofs made a waffle-like pattern on the land. Pelts hung from outdoor poles. Beans and squash were abundant. The Seneca gave thanks to their Creator. With outstretched arms, eyes raised to the sky, they joyfully thanked their God:

We thank the Great Creator for the warmth of the sun,
for the strength of our bodies. For the land that gives
us tools with which to live. May it always be so.

We thank the Great Creator for the trees that give us
shelter and fire. May it always be so.

We thank the Great Creator for the three sisters that
sustain us . . . the corn, the bean, the squash.
May it always be so.

Mary approached one of the longhouses carrying two bundles of dead wood fastened with a burden strap across her forehead. The first sister, as Mary was accustomed to calling her, appeared from the longhouse.

"Dehewamus, not two bundles, only one. You need only carry your share. Each bundle is a gift from the tree. This one shall be mine."

She took the bundle from her and placed it by an ever

53

present fire. Then she took Mary's hand and led her to a near-by stream. They passed many Seneca on their walk. Men together on one side. Women on the other. Some of the women gestured a greeting and Mary nodded in return. When they got to the stream they sat on the ground.

Mary no longer used benches or stumps. The ground, the earth was now her friend. For almost three years her sisters had shown her the Seneca ways. She was peaceful now, at rest with her fate. She was treated kindly and with respect. Her work consisted of tending babies and carrying wood. Occasionally she would help drag a deer or elk carcass into camp for carving.

"Dehewamus, it is time for talk. The Delaware who now share our camp are our brothers. Sheninjee, a good Indian, must now take a wife. The council of women have decided and you have been chosen."

Mary looked up in alarm. "Chosen? To be a wife? To a . . . ? But, Sister, I am only seventeen. I am not ready!"

Mary was surprised at her own outburst. She had immediately felt disgust at the thought of being an Indian's wife.

The sister put a finger to Mary's mouth to hush her.

"It is our way. We will be leaving at the new sun to follow the way of the spring geese. Sheninjee goes the way of the robin in winter. You will go with him."

Mary shook her head and tried to say no.

"You are Seneca, Dehewamus. You must obey the Seneca way."

Mary was overwhelmed, but she kept her peace. The sister touched her arm affectionately and left her to her thoughts. She looked to each side of her, to run, to go back, but she wasn't good with direction. She knew she'd be lost. A red ant struggled with a captured, almost dead caterpillar, dragging it, tossing it over stones and twigs, then changing direction, looking for a path. Mary waited until the ant was on safer ground with a clear path before it. A silent rage poured though her as the soft heel of her moccasin crushed both creatures into the ground. She checked and the ant still moved. She squashed it again, grinding it into the earth, ripping it from its flattened prey. The ant tried to fight back and flipped its twisted body back and forth. Mary watched it slowly die, then fell to the ground and cried.

"Oh, Mama. It's so hard. The river still shows me with your hair. With Papa's eyes. But my daydreams are gone, my life taken cruelly away from me, yet saved for my memory. I can not stand to be an Indian's wife. I can not stand to have Indian children. What should I do, Mama? Oh, God, what should I do?"

After a moment she dried her tears, resigned once again to the path ahead of her. She made sure no one was listening so she could practice her prayers.

"Our Father, who be in Heaven. We thank you. . . . We thank you for the trees . . . oh, Mama, I'm forgetting the words! Jane, Tom, Jesse, John."

She stood and walked back to the camp.

"And Matt. Jemison."

She was taken to Sheninjee at dusk by her two sisters. Sheninjee sat by one of the fires in the longhouse, complacent, reserved. He looked different from the Seneca she was used to. He was as lean, but shorter, with a softness about him she was sure he wasn't proud of.

Sheninjee welcomed her to his fire and the two sat in peace into the night. Their marriage was not what she expected. There was no ceremony. No courtship. Sheninjee seemed to accept her immediately as the one he would care for, be a companion to, and who would bear strong children.

She remembered spying on her parents once as she heard the rhythmic knocking of their cot against the farm house wall. Mary felt afraid of such an act. She couldn't imagine this stranger, this Indian, pushing his seed into her. She craved love, and gentleness.

"We must leave before the sun is high," he said.

"You are my wife, now. A Delaware by marriage, but a Seneca. Our children will be Seneca. They will inherit their mother's name."

Sheninjee asked her to kneel in front of him. Other families who shared their longhouse paid no attention. Gently he sowed his seed, as she had done on the farm, carefully pushing and covering the soil.

Sheninjee led her to her new home and she quietly followed. In some ways she feared him. Her last three years had been spent with women and children. Men and women seldom shared time together. Seeing Sheninjee and being with him reminded her of her past. Her mind wanted to hate him for being an Indian, a man, a warrior. But he was always tender with her. He never raised his voice or looked down on her and she respected him. Soon she would have a baby. The thought of being a mother frightened her. She would never want her child taken or killed. She couldn't bear it the way her mother had.

Now that her belly was growing she realized she felt a new anger, one directed at another. She was angry that her mother let go, that she didn't fight. She pounded her stomach with white-knuckled fists. Her baby must die. Die before it had time to suffer. She pounded and clawed at her skin, desperately trying to reach the seed within her. Sheninjee saw her anger and firmly grasped her arms to her side. She twisted and jerked away pounding again and again. Sheninjee wrapped his arms around hers and her body, holding her close to him, quietly containing her until her exhaustion made her slump in his embrace. Slowly he moved one hand to her rounded front.

"The warrior in you needs to find its way," he said.

She glared at him, but slowly warmed to his gentleness. He was easy to talk to, as Jesse had been; and strong, like Tom. But there was more. He had a way with her, a warm breeziness that defied her anger and the hatred of the Indian in him.

"I'll tell you truth," she said, and she knew it was safe to do so. "I hate my mother for letting me go to the Indians! For not letting me die with her."

She waited silently for his reaction. His dark brown eyes kept their calm and he warmly took her hand in his.

"Your mother was brave," he said. "She knew you would live and be strong. She thought of the generations to follow, as her generation had spent their time on earth. She saved you from yourself, Dehewamus, from your own weakness. You must thank her."

For a long time they studied their reflections in each other. Though Mary felt old and torn, the image in Sheninjee's eyes was the same as it was at the river on her father's farm. And Sheninjee's eyes seemed to shine with love for her, almost the way she once dreamed a man would look at her. She hadn't changed. She only felt tired as she steadied herself in Sheninjee's arms. Quietly he lifted her, and quietly he carried her home.

That winter the snow fell so long that often one door of the longhouse was blocked with drifts. The hunters had trouble finding game, and those they found had often frozen or starved to death. Though everyone shared the catch, food was scarce. Mary felt that the child within her suffered from the lack of food. When spring arrived and the berries blossomed, the camp rejoiced. A festival welcoming the new season lasted days and into the night. Men and women danced in a way new to Mary. They rejoiced to a Creator who gave them all good things. Mary ate heartily. She tried to fill the void of winter with as much of the spring fruits as she could consume.

With a kind elder woman beside her for guidance and attention, Mary went to the birthing boughs. It was a crude shelter designed for limited privacy and the easing of birth. Beneath Mary's feet were layers of soft cones and pine needles. These would soak up the blood of birth. Above her were strong, flexible branches to take hold of while she pushed her child from her body.

Her body was determined to resist and she writhed in pain. The camp heard her screams and the echoes of her childhood disappeared in the brush. Finally her cries stopped as she felt the tiny form slip from her in its final push to freedom. Mary emerged from the boughs sweaty, sick, exhausted. The Seneca woman followed her out carrying an infant now wrapped in a skin. The elder checked the baby from top to bottom. She put her ear to the baby's chest to listen.

"Is it a girl? A baby girl?"

The elder nodded and again checked the child. After a moment she handed it to Mary, shaking her head and leaving her. Mary was pleased with herself as she held her daughter.

"I shall name you Jane. Jane Jemison"

She looked down at the baby, tried to rouse it.

"Wake up, little Jane. Jane Jemison, wake up. It's time to give thanks."

The baby didn't move or make a sound. Concerned, Mary tried harder.

"Jane! What's wrong with you child? Wake up! You are named after my mother. You will always be with me. Wake up, Jane. Jane! Mama!"

She fell to her knees and cradled her dead child, her dead mother.

Mary stood by the outdoor fire warming herself from the chill of fall. Her body was thinner, drawn around her. Strands of her long hair glimmered from the fire light as it draped her curved and solid arms. She smelled the deadness of the leaves and heard the honk of fleeing geese above her. Her thoughts were of another time, another place. A time she could barely remember. A place she wasn't sure ever existed. The elder came to her at the fire and placed a loving hand on her shoulder.

"At the new sun you will go with Sheninjee, to the fort at the two rivers."

Mary didn't respond. She hardly saw Sheninjee anymore. The warriors of the camp spent their days hunting and fishing. On days when the camp was stocked with food they played war games to maintain their readiness. Other days they took young boys to the forest to teach them the way of the woods. At night they shared talk of his hunt or the games of the men, but she distanced herself from him.

The elder continued. "Your sickness has been long. You will go and help carry skins for trading."

Mary blinked her eyes as if finally awakening to the elder's words.

"But, the British?"

"Yes, the British now inhabit the fort. But we are a great Nation. We keep the peace."

Mary unconsciously nodded. She had never seen the British. At council fires the men sat in a circle, the women forming another circle around them. It was the women's job to listen and remember the stories, so they could be passed on to generations after them. The women's voices were equal to the men's. She had heard of the British there. They were white. They wanted land.

Mary went with her husband as she was instructed. She had felt angry with Sheninjee, as if her baby's death was somehow his fault. Being with him, sharing, talking, made her realize that her anger was another part of her sickness. The elder was right in sending her. Her loneliness and despair were overwhelming to her. She needed to breathe the life of the forest and feel her spirit again.

As Mary and Sheninjee neared the fort in their canoe, Mary's memory jumped to consciousness. The sight of the fort sent her mind into panic. She was white with fear. She searched beside her for the pouch of scalps, but, except for the skins, the canoe was empty.

Warriors in another canoe full of trading furs followed them to the fort. Mary carried the skins with a burden strap until they were well inside. Then the men took the skins and left her as they went to trade.

The fort was bustling. British soldiers stood guard in the turrets, their bright red uniforms blazing in the sun. French, whites of all classes, and Seneca milled around the central area, mixing and mingling without hostility or tension.

All eyes were on Mary. White men and women, Dutch, Irish and English approached her in wonder. They looked her up and down as she did them. A man with a slight resemblance to her father startled her as he came closer.

"Well, Lass. Would you be one of those Indian captives?"

Mary was shocked by his speech, his manner. A woman dressed in layers of white turned Mary toward her.

"Please, dear. Are you a captive? Are you white?"

Mary nodded, then shook her head. She was confused, annoyed. Why was it alright for all of them to be here? Why wasn't she with them? Why wasn't her family here? Her family. She thought for a moment that maybe they could be here. Maybe the scalps she remembered were a cruel joke to keep her from running. Maybe her Pa had managed to escape and save the family.

Another man, gruffer than the first and slightly farther away, slapped a friend next to him on the back.

"By, George! I think she is white!"

"We can be saving you, girl," said the first man. "You can come with us, find your people. Would you like that?"

Mary looked at him dumbfounded. Could she really leave? Just walk away with them and be white again?

Could she go back and relearn the ways of white people?

She wondered what it would be like. She wondered if she could teach them to share the way Indians shared.

"Look at her," the first man said to the others. "She needs to go with her own kind. We can get her away. What do ya say, lads?"

The second man shouted out as the others nodded their approval. "I'd be willin' to help. Got me a small boat out by the water. Come with us, girl!"

He took her arm and she hardly resisted. In some ways it was as if they were taking her captive. She didn't want to fight. She was white. She could never really be an Indian. She needed to go home. But where was home? Who would be there for her? Sheninjee was her husband. Her sisters loved her. The women of the village were her friends.

Suddenly another hand grabbed her arm and she watched the whites around her retreat in fear. Sheninjee pulled her with him as she stared at the gathering. She could hear their mumbles. "Should we follow?" "Get your boat, we'll help her." "We'll meet you." Sheninjee pulled her faster and made her jump into the canoe. He paddled quickly, checking behind him to be sure no one threatened their course. When he felt safe he turned Mary toward him.

"You are of the Iroquois," he said. "A Seneca. No whites will ever harm you."

The love in his eyes was calming to her. She wasn't sure, but she felt she might love him. He had never hurt her. He showed all respect for her as Indian men should. She had tried to have his baby. He was all she had. How wrong she had been! He was her man of the woods, her provider and protector.

As he paddled their way back to camp she watched the last colored leaves fall from the trees. As they swirled in the air and rested on the rivers current she decided she did love Sheninjee. And she knew they would try again to have a child.

⊰⊱⊰⊱⊰⊱

Mary cried out from the birthing boughs. Again the elder tended to her. It was an ordeal for Mary. Her body was slight and the physical pain of birth mixed with the anguish over her lost child. When it was over, she came out of the boughs afraid. She needed this baby. She needed a part of her to grow

61

and survive. The elder followed her, checking the baby as she did before. Mary didn't look. She didn't want to know.

The elder tried to hand her the baby, but Mary refused.

"Fine," said the woman. "A warrior. Take him."

"He's fine? Alive?"

"Yes, yes." The elder nodded. "Take him. Go to the river and wash his stains."

Mary carefully took the baby in her arms and the elder gave her a loving shove toward the river.

"Go! Jogo!"

Mary cradled him gently as she washed him and wrapped him in a skin. His blue eyes twinkled as he struggled to open them. His skin was white and his wisps of hair sparkled red-gold in the sun.

"Your name will be Tom. Tom Jemison. A man of the woods. A farmer."

She looked to the trees swaying in the breeze, then raised Tom above her, presenting him.

"Papa? This is your grandson. His name is your name. His blood is my blood."

She cradled the baby again, crying as she looked at him.

"I'll love him as no other. He'll be a man afraid of nothing, save his God. He'll be my strength, my tree, the son of Sheninjee."

Mary was old enough to help in the corn fields now. She watched as other Seneca women planted in single rows. As one finished, she would sit and wait until each had completed her row so that no one's labor was greater than another's. Tom was on her back, on a cradle board Sheninjee had carved from a fallen oak tree. It was decorated with carved and painted hawks and corn tassels. Around the edges were painted trees and different colored skies. It was special to her, A creation from Sheninjee. The molded handle was perfect for toting or hanging and the smoothness was comfortable on her back.

The elder in charge of the fields took the board from Mary's back and hung it on a nearby tree. Other cradle boards, all decorated differently, hung from different branches, swaying in the wind, rocking the children with gentle nature. This was the true way to grow. The babies kept a calmness within them, their eyes and ears alert and thankful for the sounds of birds and flowing water and rustling leaves and dancing sunlight. No chopping or man-made words or noisy anvils or angry sounds. These were the children of the sun and the earth. The elder pointed Mary toward a young woman planting seed.

"Crossing Star will teach you to plant."

"But I know how," Mary said. "I used to . . ."

"Crossing Star will teach!" The elder gave her a slight push. "Go!"

Mary joined Crossing Star, but was angry with the elder for not trusting her knowledge. The woman first showed her a small hand tool, a hoe, made out of wood. She motioned to Mary to copy her as she hoed a small area, then made a furrow with her fingers. Mary copied, but awkwardly. Her farm had been plowed by a disk and horses. Her furrows were made with a hoe large enough to hold while standing.

Crossing Star took the seeds in her hands and slowly placed six in a furrow. Mary was shocked. Her lip trembled as she also took the seeds and counted six. With cloudy eyes she gently put them in the ground and covered them cautiously, wincing as if she'd hurt them.

She buried them, six at a time, while Crossing Star watched and approved. Again and again six seeds were planted and covered. Again and again Mary shook and trembled. Six seeds in a furrow, then dirt for their grave. Six. And six more. Suddenly Mary threw the seeds to the ground and stamped them into the earth.

"Like this! Plant them like this!"

Crossing Star tried to touch her, to comfort her, but Mary

was lost in her resurfaced grief. The elder motioned for Crossing Star to wait.

"Crush them!" Mary was scattering the seed now, darting and racing to each spot, crushing them and grinding them again and again.

"This corn will never grow. It shouldn't grow! Let it die! Let it die. Let it die."

She threw herself on the ground and hugged the earth with all her memory.

"Let it die," she sobbed. "It needs to die. Please. Let it die so I can live again."

Crossing Star knelt beside her and stroked her hair.

"The salt from your body is good for the earth, Dehewamus."

"No! No! Please, leave me alone."

"Your feeling is good, my sister."

Mary bolted and clutched Crossing Star's dress.

"You don't know my feeling. You are not my sister! Was your family killed? Were you left with no one? With a shattered heart? With nightmares for company each night? Is their blood in your eyes and death in every spring? You don't know how I feel!"

She relaxed her grip and let her body slump back to the ground.

"Go away. Let me die with the corn."

Crossing Star stayed and kept her hand on Mary. Though Mary wanted her to leave, the warmth of her touch was soothing and real.

"Hear me, Dehewamus. As a child of six harvests I, too, lost my family. I smelled the blood of my father, the stink of my brother's gnawed bones. The white man killed them with white dogs, a man of white skin named Frank-lin ordered the dogs from across the ocean. They were killed then left to be eaten by the dogs. My perch in a tree saved me from their game. But I do not wish to die. My wish is for my children. The children of my future, to live so they may live."

Mary slowly eased her embrace of the earth. She had a son, a child to live for. Yes, he had Indian blood, but he was also a part of her. She raised her eyes to view Tom still swaying from his branch. She wanted him to live, to become a man. She needed to live for him.

She sat up and dried her tears, the tears that watered her soul. The gentle Crossing Star continued to stroke and soothe her. She did understand and Mary thought her beautiful because of or in spite of her pain.

Crossing Star stood and offered Mary her hand. Mary searched her eyes and found friendship and caring. These people were, indeed, her family. She let the woman help her to her feet and then, as though Heaven opened to her and her Creator touched her heart, she embraced her Indian sister with all the unharvested love within her.

The women stayed in the field through the day, stopping only to feed their children or wait for others to catch up. Mary felt more at home, more alive than she had for seven years.

6

"It's time to give thanks for the day, young Tom." Mary hummed Tom's tune as she sprang from the longhouse at dawn. Six month old Tom was cradled in her arms as she carried him to the stream. She held him, took his hand, and looked up toward the sun.

"Our Father, the Great Creator. Thank you for the three sisters, the corn, the bean, the squash. Give us daily our food and bring no enemies unto our land. Let us always live in truth. Amen."

Sheninjee had followed her and listened to her words. As he approached her he ignored the baby, but he was sensitive and caring with her.

"We go again to the great fort, to prepare for the season of snow. You will come."

"I will go, my husband, but I wish to stay in the canoe."

Sheninjee gave her a knowing look.

"If that is your wish, let it be so. The trip will be hard. The cold of the season greets us early. Prepare well."

Mary sat with Tom as Sheninjee and two Seneca brothers returned from the fort. She smiled at his return. He was truly her husband and her friend. The fort and the people in it were a past she had not wanted to see again.

"Dehewamus, you must go to the land of your sisters,

66

toward the bright star that guides us and the land of great waters. Our brothers will take you there."

"And you, Sheninjee? You will come, too?"

"No. I will stay to hunt as our people will need food. We cannot go to our home of the season. There is new trouble for our Nation. I will join you when the season turns warm."

Mary looked at him lovingly as he placed his hand on her shoulder.

"Our home will be stocked with the three sisters for your return, my husband."

Sheninjee waved to his brothers and disappeared into the forest. Mary was already anxious for his return. The two brothers paddled the canoe as far up river as they could go. When they shored the canoe was hidden so that any other traveller who was not Indian would not know its whereabouts.

Mary loaded Tom on her back on his cradle board and carried their provisions with a burden strap. Tom was heavier now, but Mary's back was strong, strengthened by many loads of corn and wood. They continued their journey on foot. The two brothers led the way carrying nothing but knives and tomahawks. They had to have their hands free for battle or intruding animals. The rains of late fall began and grew colder as they headed north. The trees were almost bare and Mary could smell snow in the air. The cold rain soaked her clothing and chilled Tom into a constant cry. Still she kept a quick step, kept pace with her Seneca brothers. She had learned to move her legs in short, fast steps as long strides could be tiring and throw her off balance. In spite of her burden she was able to forge streams and plod through swamps in step with the men. When balance was needed on a log crossing a stream, Mary kept hers proudly.

As night drew in around them they built a small fire, one that could stay hidden from possible enemies. Mary had only a wet blanket to warm her and her son.

Daybreak was cold and clear and they started their pace

early. The constant run helped to warm their muscles. They came upon two horses grazing in a clearing and Mary watched as the men gracefully waved their arms and used cooing sounds to soothe the horses into capture. Each man climbed astride a horse and motioned for Mary to follow. She wanted to tell them that she knew how to ride a horse and could ride double to speed their trip, but she held back. On journeys and in war the men were in charge. It was the Seneca way.

They spent a cold night shivering in darkness. Mary felt her skin harden from the scorching cold. A light snow started falling and left a dust at Mary's feet. They had almost finished eating when they heard the long cry of a cougar. The men jumped up, sniffing the air and straining to listen. One cougar could mean more. The horses pulled at their ties and broke away. The brothers followed their tracks into the forest and Mary waited, an inch of snow now around her.

At daybreak she still waited. She fed twigs to the small fire and watched as the sun made its path through the blueness of the winter sky to a point above her. Her brother's tracks were long covered by the snow. She scanned the forest openings for any sign and she wondered then what kind of trouble Sheninjee spoke of. She didn't know of any new hostilities, but it had been some time since she was at a council fire. She decided it was best to make her own way to find her sisters. The provisions on her back would not last very long and she had no weapons to hunt for food. She loaded Tom and her burden strap and continued north.

The snow came harder, in small pellets, piling and packing on the ground before her. She wished she had remembered to bring the special snow shoes Sheninjee had made. He had warned her of a hard cold season, but she thought they'd be well south.

In front of her was a small deserted village. She approached it cautiously. She had been carrying Tom in her arms to shelter him from the cold, but she put him back on his board in case they needed to run. She, too, had to keep her arms free in case of danger.

"We must find food, my son. We need our strength."

She searched the ground and the bark houses for food. She could tell by the different war-poles that this was a Delaware village. Though also ten feet tall, they were different from the Seneca poles. Their markings for war and days were longer, more pronounced. She knew she would find food. The Delaware always buried food in different places, in case it was needed by a passing warrior. The snow made it harder. She crawled on her hands and knees searching for small mounds of rocks in the snow. Finally a small pile peeked out at her. She carefully uncovered the burying place and pulled out stored honey and herbs.

"It is the Delaware way," she said.

She and Tom huddled beneath a shelter of boughs while they ate and watched the snow. She didn't trust the houses. Sheninjee had told her that trouble always came to houses first. The safest place was away from the houses, in shelter, but able to view the surroundings.

She guarded through the night, watching Tom sleep in her lap and rubbing his skin to warm him. She blew on him with a breath warmed by the will to survive. As she watched him she remembered her father and wondered if he knew the forest as well as Sheninjee. He had never taught her how to survive alone. Her young Tom looked like her father, but she vowed he would be different. He would know the ways of the forest and would know how to survive.

The next morning was clear and crisp. The sun on the fresh white snow blinded Mary on her trek. She tried to hum Tom's song to keep her mind off the cold, but she stumbled on the tune. She settled instead for a Seneca song that seemed to fill her with new strength.

She reached the banks of a river. Ice chunks flowed with the current and Mary knew it would only be days before the river froze. She checked for a canoe but didn't find one. She paced back and forth searching for a place to cross. She could wait until it froze, but her provisions wouldn't hold out that long. She also couldn't trust that the weather would stay cold long enough. She had to cross.

She chose her spot and, holding Tom over her head, she waded into the swift current. The current was stronger than she had expected. Once and then again she almost slipped and lost Tom. Then, suddenly, she slipped and went under. Tom's board was floating down the river, rocking and crashing against the ice chunks. Mary surfaced and frantically looked for her baby. She spotted him some ways away from her and she began a frenzied swim to rescue him. She slapped and splashed at the water, gulping for air, spitting out the coldness.

The snow began again. It was that blinding kind of storm that comes quickly and passes just as fast. Baby Tom cried out in a frightened wail. Mary followed him in the current, sometimes following only the sound of his voice. As she followed she untied the deer hide from her gown and pulled off her outer dress. She struggled defiantly to tie them together, using her teeth to hold one end, and splashed at the water with her free hand. Tom still cried and the awful sound pierced her heart with fear.

Once the makeshift "lasso" was fashioned and secure, she tried to fling it forward to catch on the cradle board. The first try didn't come close. She pulled it in, splashed forward and tried again. She was a little closer, but it was hard to see. She splashed and kicked harder, screaming Tom's name. The scream turned into a Seneca war whoop as she flung her lasso again. A piece of the dress caught one end of the board. She held tight trying to draw the board back toward her against the current. The distance between them lessened, but she still couldn't reach him. She stretched her body as far as she could. She almost had him. Almost. Almost. But the board tore loose from the dress. Mary tugged at an empty catch. She lunged for the carrier with a strength only a mother has and went under the water. The board spun in the current as Tom screamed. A moment. Another. And she surfaced with the board in hand. She grasped it tightly though her hands were frozen and blue.

She made it to the opposite shore and slumped in exhaustion. Her outer dress had been lost in the current. Her son was wet and freezing. She dragged the board to cover and surveyed her surroundings. Her shivering was uncontrollable making her teeth crack together and her eyes blur from the tremors. She smelled smoke and strained for its direction. She pressed Tom against her chest for warmth and stumbled into the forest.

"Come. The smoke is wood. We must find it."

The snow continued. Mary's hands and face were icy sculptures. She pushed her way through snow laden brush and icy needles jabbed at her every step.

A small cabin, smoke streaming from its chimney, made her almost cry out in relief. She cautioned herself, remembering Sheninjee's words about danger. She saw no tracks in the snow, no horses, no weapons. She crept closer and listened for sounds of life. Baby Tom cried out in his coldness. Quickly Mary broke an icy branch and put it in his mouth to chew on. She readied her burdens for flight. She would run if she had to, but she had to find warmth and food. She inched closer to the cabin. The wind pushed the white smoke downward and it circled her in its dance. Even the smoke felt warm to her. She took her stance at the door. If death lurked inside it would be a quicker end than freezing at the hands of nature.

She pounded once. Then again. Again and again and again. When the door cracked open she saw the surprised faces of two black men. Their eyes were wide with wonder. She eyed them the same way. These men were darker than any she had seen. If they were Indian they were from a tribe she didn't know. She didn't speak or move. She let them gaze upon her until they could decide her fate. The door opened wider and the men let her pass. She nodded to each as she entered and went quickly to turn her back to the fire. If the next moments were meant for staring or talking, she intended to warm herself and her child while they were doing it.

One of the men crossed the cabin floor timidly sitting in a rocking chair that faced the fire. The other took a seat on a bench by a wooden table making sure that he, too, faced Mary and the fire. The trio stayed like this for several minutes. No words. No gestures. Just a silent wonder of differences and like needs. The man on the bench finally offered Mary some corn bread which she quickly broke into pieces to feed Tom. As if by instinct Tom, too, kept his silence.

Sure that she was safe from danger, Mary unpacked her provisions, dried skins and rags by the fire, warmed her son, and rested on the floor. The cabin smells were familiar to her. On the mantle was a bible. She didn't understand why black Indians would have a bible. Or why they would prefer to sit in chairs instead of on the solid earth. She looked for weapons, but saw only a gun by the door. The room was well stocked with corn and honey, herbs, roots and beans. She saw no sign of a woman's presence. She wondered where the Indian women were who farmed for these men.

They sat silent into the night. Mary lay Tom on a skin near the fire and the black men watched him fall asleep. As if it was a signal to them, they quietly rose from their chairs and went to their beds to sleep. Mary felt their eyes on her as she laid down next to Tom and joined him in thankful rest.

The next morning one of the men awoke with a start. He looked toward the fire, but Mary wasn't there. The fire blazed hot as though freshly tended, but Mary wasn't there. He looked under the table, under the chair. Just as he was about to open the door he did a double-take to the hook near the window. There was a smiling Tom, snug on his cradle board, eyes twinkling at the stranger. Tom looked at him. He looked at Tom. The door opened and Mary looked at both. She carried more wood to the fire and deposited it directly on the floor.

The man moved toward her slowly, as if approaching a wounded animal. He tried to pick up a few pieces of wood looking at her helpfully, but she motioned him away.

The other man awoke and pushed himself up on his elbow. The two men eyed each other for a moment, looked at Tom hanging near the window, and shrugged. The first man wiped a hand on his trousers and extended it to Mary.

"My name be Theodore! After the master that sired me! Folks mostly call me Teddy."

Mary looked at his hand and nodded. Teddy sheepishly pulled his hand back and wiped it again on his trousers. He pointed to the man still in bed.

"This here be Calvin, my friend."

Mary heard a pride in his voice as he named his friend. She turned to acknowledge Calvin, then turned back to the fire.

"We be runaways," Teddy said.

Mary looked at him confused. Runaways from what? Did they run from other Indians or from whites?

"Slaves," Calvin added. "From a place called Virginny."

Mary shook her head. She had never heard of slaves or Virginny.

"We was good slaves. Just, well, the master died. Had to run then." Teddy was childlike as he spoke to Mary, but Mary didn't answer. She didn't know some of the words he used.

"You and yo' child are welcome to stay. Me and Cal agreed to it."

Mary was pensive. "I will work for you, to pay my way."

Teddy smiled, obviously elated at the thought of company. "That's good! We'll need help with some planting in the spring. . . if you'll be staying that long?"

"Corn?"

"Corn."

Mary approved. "But," she said. "The masters you spoke of. There will be more? To run away from?"

Teddy's smile turned to a look of pain as he sat on the

bench near her. Cal stepped forward and answered for him.

"The masters will always be behind us. And when we run, we run to others."

"But who are these masters? Other dark men?"

"White men. White, like you."

Mary spread her hand, studying the color, then held it close to Teddy's.

"Where I am from we have no masters, no. . .slaves."

Calvin looked at Teddy, then back to Mary. "If you're speaking the truth, that's the place we want to go."

"When I see my brothers, I will ask them if it can be."

Mary pounded ground corn meal, baked bread and corn pone and fed her new family. The men ate at the table, but she and Tom still preferred the floor. When they had finished she took Tom in her arms and stood in front of the fireplace. Taking Tom's hand, she closed her eyes and raised her head toward the ceiling. The men looked on, unaware of what she was doing.

Mary spoke softly. "We thank you, Great Creator, for our new day."

Realizing that she was praying, Teddy and Calvin looked at each other and jumped up to bow their heads as Mary continued.

"We thank you for the trees that give us the gift of warmth. We thank you for the sister, the corn, that gives us strength and sustains us. We thank you for the snow that blankets the soil and makes it ready for a new season."

She paused, opened her eyes that now twinkled with gladness, and looked at the men.

"Amen?" Asked Teddy.

Mary smiled. "Amen."

Tom grew stronger through the long winter. Mary made him and the men clothes from deer hides that Calvin provided and she taught Teddy how to find wood that the earth didn't need. She enjoyed watching the men play with her son, especially Teddy, who Tom seemed to like the most. They lived as a family through the coldness and, often, Mary's heart filled with sadness and old grief as the smells of the cabin filled her senses and revived her memory. She felt these men were her brothers, their playfulness and companionship at times moved her to tears. She thought of John and Jesse, wondered what happened after their escape. She understood now why the Seneca had hurt her family. She didn't accept it, but she understood.

She and the men would take turns telling stories each night, to pass the time, to warm themselves by the fire, and to know each other. Calvin's stories were always filled with strange sounding characters dressed in funny clothes, swaying their bodies or acting like animals. His descriptions even made Tom giggle sometimes and Calvin would exaggerate a pose or a face to make him giggle more.

Teddy's stories were almost always serious. He spoke of hardship and whips, and lost family. At times Mary chided herself for ever thinking her life had been hard. Her short captivity before her adoption into the Seneca tribe seemed trivial compared to his lifetime of pain. She realized how happy she was as a Seneca, how peaceful and caring they were. She felt sorry for Teddy, but she also felt proud of him. He had survived and fought for his life, and it was he who opened the door the widest when she knocked.

Mary's stories were Seneca stories, stories that told of good and evil, life and death. She spoke of the earth as mother, and the sun as father. She told them of the three sisters, the corn, bean, and squash, born of the union between the sun and the earth. She spoke of the sacred Corn Maiden, and the evil of destroying corn. She told them of the shining path that led to Heaven, a path that all must sometime walk. The road in the sky was a forked one. The good went one way to peace and happiness. The evil went the other and travelled forever in search of peace. When the cold wind chilled them, she told them it was the bear, one of the beasts of Gaoh, God of the winds. The bear was from the North, the fawn, the South. The East wind was the moose, and the West was the panther.

They passed their stories to each other and kept alive their history.

When the fawn came in spring to help melt the snow, Mary planted her corn seed as a Seneca woman. Teddy stood guard with a gun, unable to understand that she was in no danger from Indians. To him she was a white woman and he knew stories of white women being taken by Indians. He couldn't plant while he guarded so the help Mary gave was actually no help at all. Occasionally she'd stop to look at him and wave. He'd wave back, check on Tom playing or swinging from a tree, and then he'd solemnly return to his vigil.

When the corn was high, Mary and Calvin harvested while Teddy maintained his guard. Mary was much faster than Calvin, used to a pace that was efficient, but not tiring. Calvin struggled to keep up with her as she carried her bundles of corn from the field. Eighteen month old Tom played by the corn stacks while Mary separated her bundles. She gave the men two ears for every one of hers.

The leaves turned the forest to vibrant color and the corn was gone.

Mary, Teddy and Calvin sat on the floor with Tom on Teddy's lap. The harvest was done. They were prepared for winter.

"Me and Cal gonna leave in the spring," Teddy said. "Gotta move away from the cold, maybe find family, black folks. Gotta go somewhere safe."

Mary's eyes filled with sadness, but she knew it was time for this change. She had family to return to and she knew she was strong enough now to make the journey.

Ted continued, his eyes lowered. "We been real proud to

work with you. Proud to guard and live with you and the boy. May even . . . miss you some."

"No need to hide your eyes, Ted-dy. You gave me good work, good payment of corn. You have been friends to me and my son. The Seneca will not forget."

Teddy nodded shyly, then chuckled.

"Still seems funny to me, you bein' Indian and my guarding you. Musta seemed pretty foolish to you."

Mary touched his hand. "The Great Creator is pleased with your work. Your path will be a good one."

A tear escaped Teddy's eye and he quickly brushed it away.

"Me and Cal been talkin'. This here cabin will be yours now. Ain't really no gift, nothin' to smile about. Weren't even ours to begin with. But we give it to you, just the same."

"I will also be leaving," Mary said. "I must find the village of my sisters, near a great falls. There I will wait word from my husband."

Calvin leaned forward. He loved travel stories and seemed to know about many places he'd never been.

"Is it a great falls with three tiers?"

Mary shook her head, she didn't know. She remembered her sisters telling her it was near the Chosen place and some days walk from the mighty water of Niagawa.

"Hmmm . . . a large village? The Eerie quois, or somethin' similar?"

"Yes," Mary answered. "Near the largest of our villages."

"Think I know of the place. Beyond the traders. Up the river that runs backwards. Yep, it sure do. Ain't never heard or seen nothin' like it. All the rivers we followed run like this." He motioned up to down. "This one, it go the other way."

Mary nodded. "Then I am on the right path. I come from the land that starts the great river."

Calvin leaned back. Mary always thought when he leaned that way that he should have a pipe in his mouth, much like she'd seen the Seneca men do when they were thinking deeply.

77

"Why, that be near a hundred miles, maybe more."

"And my village, near the falls?"

"Don't know. Maybe, maybe four hundred, even five."

He looked at her hard, incredulously.

"How you 'spect to make that trip?"

"Don't worry, my brother, Calvin. It is only a path of life. I'll walk like I walked the one that brought me here."

She watched Cal lean back again, looking like a chief. His eyes said he doubted her. Teddy seemed more aware of her strengths.

"I'll tell you the way to go," he said. "To the traders, best I can. But from there you got to find it on your own. You're lookin' for a place just before the river runs outta strength. A place near another country called Canada. We'd take ya, if we could. But that ain't no place for people colored like us."

Mary looked at some different colored herbs in her hand and ground them together in her palm.

"Don't know what color is supposed to be where. The leaves turn color, all colors, beautiful colors, then they die. In the hot season, the leaves are all green, dancing on the branches, working together to protect and feed those that hunger. I know no people who are green like the leaves. Seems only when they start being different colors, that's when they die."

She ground the herbs some more and tossed them into the fire. The scent filled the room with a peaceful friendliness. Teddy stood up and took the bible from the mantle.

"I think it's my turn to lead."

Mary and Calvin nodded their approval. Teddy took his place in front of the fireplace. He didn't open the book because he couldn't read, but he kept it in front of him while Mary, Cal and Tom held hands and they all gave thanks to the Great Creator.

The snow blew against the cabin and the smoke streamed from the chimney as Teddy romped with Tom on the floor. Tom's laughter filled the silence of winter as Cal watched and smiled. Mary stared out the window whispering the names of her lost family. As she watched, a deer stumbled into view, skinny and half-starved. It walked a drunken path across the field, fell to its knees, and froze to death. Mary felt a cold chill go through her as she watched it die. Like the animals the Indians, too, would die from the cold and lack of food. Frozen deer and elk would soon be buried by the snow and impossible to find until the rotting thaw exposed them.

<hr>

By spring there were buds and berries and wild flowers. Mary stood by the field holding a chattering young Tom. He was starting to talk and his words were accented with Seneca, English and, occasionally, some Irish. Tom smiled as Teddy came near and reached out to him.

"I have packed your provisions for your trip, the best I could," Mary said. "You must try to remember the ways of the forest, so you'll be safe. Sustained."

Teddy couldn't handle their parting. He was nervous, unable to meet Mary's eyes. He looked to the forest, at Tom, at anything to avoid her. Finally, as a buffer, he took Tom into his arms.

"I'll be missing our romps, little man. You're a strong boy, almost as strong as me!"

He gave Tom a soft kiss on the side of his head.

He started to hand him back to Mary, but then pulled him closer and hugged him tightly.

"My Tom is like a flower in your hands. He opens to the brightness of your eyes, the warmth flowing from your heart. From now on his name will be Thomas Theodore Jemison."

Teddy hugged him again, fighting back the tears. He reluctantly handed him back to Mary. Mary and Teddy looked at each other intently, she with affection and a smile, he with love. He kissed her softly on the cheek, then quickly turned away, grabbed his bag, and walked toward the forest.

Calvin had watched from a distance, waiting his turn. He walked up to Mary and warmly shook her hand.

"You and your son have made Teddy a man not afraid of his scars anymore."

They smiled at each other then he bent and shook Tom's hand. Mary watched as he ran to catch up with Teddy. She waved, but Teddy didn't look back.

She put Tom on his board, loaded her provisions with her burden strap, and walked away from another family.

7

It was late summer when Mary approached the cabin-like trading post. Skins hung on a rail to dry and two horses rolled in the mud of the corral to cool off. Mary was sweaty and reddened from the sun. Tom's skin browned easier than hers, but his lips were cracked and sore. Yellow jackets and mud wasps followed their sweat.

She opened the door of the cabin. Inside a bearded white man, stripped to the waist, was bound to the center post, his head hung to one side. Two Seneca danced around him, tomahawks in the air, knives scraping at the white man's skin. The Seneca laughed and whooped until they saw the white man catch Mary's eye.

She entered quietly. The white man looked at her with hope; then, realizing that she, too, was an Indian, his body slumped forward.

Mary calmly deposited Tom on the floor and placed her provisions next to him. The Seneca continued their game, jabbing, poking, scraping, laughing with delight whenever their captive cried out. Mary surveyed the cabin. There were skins, metal pots, knives, blankets, but no other people. She stepped behind the counter and found a pail of water with a ladle. The white man moaned, sometimes screamed, but Mary kept to her mission. She carried the pail closer to Tom whose eyes were wide with fear. She turned him away from the torture as he strained to watch more. The water she held in her hand for him became a more important sight and he drank his fill. When Tom's thirst was satisfied Mary took her turn, cupping her hands in the bucket and quietly drinking. When they had both finished she carefully replaced the pail and returned the ladle to its original position. She then walked to the center post and placed a hand on each Seneca's shoulder, turning them and pulling them away from their prey. One turned with his tomahawk raised, ready to strike at her. But she stood her ground and he backed away. The captive pleaded with her.

"Water, please. Some water."

Mary nodded to him. As the Seneca watched she retrieved the pail and held the ladle for the bound captive as he drank. When he was finished she again replaced the pail.

She came back to the post and approached the attacking Seneca. Watching his eyes, she abruptly took his knife away. He was shocked and tried to grab it back, but her look, the unquestionable determination in her eyes, made him once again back off from her. She glanced at the other Seneca who had not yet made a move. As soon as she turned toward him he took three steps away from her and the captive.

Mary stood squarely in front of the bound man and reached around behind him with the knife. Her body almost touched his and his face was full of fear and confusion. He winced as the knife cut the rope, then looked at her with silent gratitude. Mary motioned to him to leave, but he wasn't sure what it meant. She motioned again. He tested his boundaries by taking a few steps toward the door and watching the reactions of his captors. Sure he was safe, he darted out the door.

Mary watched him until he was well into the forest. When she was sure he was far enough away, she turned to her Seneca brothers. She handed the knife back to the first Seneca and sniffed his breath as he took it. She turned away in disgust and spat on the cabin floor. She sniffed the breath of the other Seneca and shook her head in despair.

Quietly she picked up Tom and her provisions and went to the door. She thought again and turned to speak to them.

"The Seneca Nation is a nation of peace. Do not let the white man's spirits make you white men."

With that she left, leaving the Seneca standing alone in the cabin.

The leaves were just starting to change color when Mary arrived at the Seneca village. She was uncertain of her steps, cautiously looking for recognizable people. From a distance, outside the door of one of the longhouses, she spotted two women, their arms raised, heads turned up to the sun. She walked closer and could hear the end of their prayer. ". . . and the trees that protect us and give us warmth. May it always be so." They lowered their arms and their eyes as Mary and three year old Tom came still closer.

The first sister cried out. "Dehewamus!"

Mary stopped and looked at her. It had been a long time since anyone called her by her Seneca name.

"Dehewamus!" She called again.

The second said, "It is! Come! We must greet her!"

They ran to her and Mary opened her arms to greet them. "Sisters! My sisters!"

They embraced joyfully, then the sisters took her burden from her and bent down to greet Tom. They giggled at his size and manner.

"The son of Sheninjee?" the first sister asked.

"Yes," said Mary. "Sheninjee is here?"

The sisters shook their heads, looking to the ground.

"No," said the second sister. "Sheninjee took the good path to the Great Creator, more than four seasons past. The Cherokee wars caused him sickness."

Mary hung her head and sucked in the heavy sadness within her. She knew it was too late to cry or show any kind of sorrow. She had learned that the path to the Creator was a good one and that once the time of sorrow had passes, a woman's tears must not interfere. "He was a good husband."

"We must not speak his name again," the first sister reminded. "His path must not be broken. It is the Seneca way."

They stood in silent memory for a moment until the second sister broke the sadness. "Come! You are home now. We will eat!"

Mary and Tom joined them in their walk through the village. She felt at home. She recognized the smell of bark that made the longhouses. The fruit trees were bare, but she imagined them full of buds in the spring and ripe fruit in the summer. The corn stalks were high, some gone as the harvest had already begun.

"This is the place near the great falls?"

The second sister answered. "You mean the flats? Near the place the French have named Gardeau?"

"Gardeau?" Mary had heard the word before. Calvin had used it, but he wasn't sure if it meant garden and he didn't pronounce it the same way. "Gardeau? Up and down. Yes, gardeau."

The first sister had been walking and playing with Tom. She hadn't really been listening until she heard the word Gardeau.

"Gardeau? You know of him?"

"Him?"

"Yes, the one you just spoke of. Gardeau, the great warrior of the Seneca. His true name is Hiokatoo. He is more than forty winters your senior, a Chief, but the sons of the nation tease him with the name Gardeau."

Mary laughed. "I'm sorry, sister. I do not know him. I was speaking of a place."

"We are near the great falls," said the second sister. It is ten suns and moons from here."

Mary was pleased. She had found her way.

"No matter. Gardeau or not, I am home."

The three sisters joined hands as they walked through the village to their longhouse.

The house was close to forty feet long with five sections for different families. Five fires, one for each family, burned constantly, and food was always ready. Except for the morning meal there was no other set eating time. Hunger wasn't something that followed the time of day; Instead it followed the rhythm of activity. Skins lined the floor used both for sitting mats and sleeping rugs. Food hung from the ceiling in long bundles, corn, beans, squash, pumpkin and melon. Here and there the carcass of a deer or an elk hung in the smoke from the fires. Raised benches on either side served as storage areas and, when needed, sleeping areas.

Mary and her sisters sat by the fire and Tom fell fast asleep on one of the skins. They ate soft, boiled corn pone, holding it in their hands as dishes were never used.

The first sister spoke. "We heard some of your journey. From the two brothers you stopped at a trading post many suns from here. They had captured a British soldier and you stopped their game."

Mary looked down, a little afraid. She hadn't thought of the consequences of her act, only that she could not stand by and watch a man, any man, be tortured.

"I am sorry, sisters. I still can not look at such a thing. Can not accept what our warriors do."

The second sister comforted her. "You are respected, Dehewamus. Our warriors learn from birth. It is their mission. They must please the Creator with their deeds. Hiokatoo, who we spoke of, is the greatest of all warriors, and also the most ruthless. But even he has gentleness within him. You caused no shame to the Seneca. Your method was just. The council accepted your action."

Mary was alarmed. She had not imagined that her actions would be brought before the council.

"I smelled the white man's spirits on their breath," she

said. "As I remember it, it destroys our men. Destroys their goodness."

The first sister crossed her arms in judgement. "I agree with you, Dehewamus, but I fear your words. We must attend a frolic, so you may learn more of the Seneca way."

"You would send her to a frolic?" The second sister spoke as Mary had never heard her. "Would you also send her to the gauntlet? Will she, too, hold a club or a knife to attack the captives who must run? Where is your love for our sister? Does she not still carry the scars of her past? Would you open them again? From fear of words?"

"I see no harm, if Dehewamus is now a true Seneca."

The second sister stood, forcing the first sister to stand and face her.

"There is no truth in the gauntlet. White men. Black men. Running for their lives. They have no weapons. They are not deer to be hunted for food. Or bear to be chased until they tire. It is your words I fear, sister. It is you who have forgotten the Seneca way. White men taught our warriors this game. It is the white men who tell us their King is the Great Creator. The Sun King they call him. A King who lives across the ocean. It is his gauntlet our captives must endure!"

The first sister unfolded her arms, chastised and humble.

"You are right. I have forgotten. Our men act like it is a game of tradition. A Seneca game. In one moon our world changes. In each moon we forget the truth. I will guard my words."

Chastened, the first sister nodded to the other women almost reverently. As she started to leave Mary called after her.

"Sister? Wait!"

"No. She must go. She will spend time in the forest, by the water. With the creatures who roam the paths. The creatures who truly come from the Creator. She must remember. She must feel the Seneca past flow through her veins. Now we must sleep. The corn is ready. There is much to be done."

The sister laid down in her sleeping place away from Mary. Mary cuddled Tom close to her and stroked his head as he slept.

"Good night, Tom Theodore Jemison. Grandson of Tom and Jane, cousin of John, Jesse and Matt. Son of . . . Sheninjee.

Mary joined the other women in harvesting. Tom, who should have stayed with her for four summers, now played games with other Seneca boys, games played with sticks, played fiercely and competitively to please the Creator. He was different than the others, quieter, more in love with the seasons. Mary knew his place was not with women in the fields, but she felt in her heart that he also didn't truly belong with the warriors. His white skin and reddish hair set him apart immediately. She watched others look at him, but they didn't seem to notice the difference. Perhaps it was only her mind that saw him differently.

The elder in charge of the fields woke Mary from her daydream.

"Tonight you go to Hiokatoo."

The news was so sudden, so unreal, that Mary staggered backward as she stood to face the elder.

"You are young, with a child. Hiokatoo will husband you. The council of women have decided."

Mary thought about arguing, stating a position. Hiokatoo was a fierce warrior, a leader of others. He was much older than she and a true Seneca. She feared him, and she missed Sheninjee. She didn't want another man beside her, especially one who was known for his cruelty. But she had chosen the Seneca way. She thought maybe Hiokatoo's age would keep him from her bed. She retreated and nodded assent to the elder.

"Yes, I will go."

"He leaves tomorrow for battle. The Red Jackets have paid for our warrior's strength. Tonight, you are wife to Hiokatoo."

Hiokatoo was a big man, known to other men as the fastest in running, the strongest in hand play. Though he had lived nearly sixty winters only the lines in his face showed any season.

He came to Mary's sisters and presented them with a gift, a large carved bowl and wooden spoon. They accepted it and, thus, accepted Hiokatoo as Mary's husband. He came to Mary's house, as the women are the keepers of the land, and together they formed a family to share one of four fires. He stayed only long enough to acquaint himself with her body and her cooking, then left without a word or gesture. When he returned the next day, he entered with two men he called Brant and Butler, but Mary had no memory of stories about them.

They stayed and talked into the night as Mary pounded samp for their meals and mended their clothes for travel. She assumed these were men who would command battles with Hiokatoo. Tom joined them at the fire, eager to acquaint himself with the great Chief. Hiokatoo touched his hair and pulled up his chin to look at his eyes.

"You are not a Seneca. Go with your mother until your blood flows as an Indian."

Tom was heartbroken at the Chief's word, but Mary had to make him obey. He had to stay with her whenever Hiokatoo was home, but she sent him to the older boys the many days her husband was gone. War whoops sounded often now as white men fought with each other and pulled the Indians to differing sides.

Mary's few nights with Hiokatoo brought her more children. Young John, now an eight year old, looked much like his father. His hair was dark and his body sinewy. Jesse, now two, was fair-haired like Tom, but even more gentle. The baby on her back was a girl she named Nancy. Her mother once had a baby girl who died, so Mary named her baby after her.

For days and weeks the people of the village had heard the loud boom of a cannon. By now it was like a signal to the sun. Still, at dawn, when Mary was bathing Jesse in the stream, the cannon's boom made her jumpy and nervous. John and Tom, though usually at odds with each other for reasons Mary couldn't determine, sat together on the banks of the river carving a war-totem. It would carry the marks of battles, the scalps of those who lost. Mary's heart sank each time she saw it, but it was now the Seneca way and she had to accept. Another boom, unlike the usual blasts, startled Mary again. The first sister rushed to her.

"Dehewamus, we must make preparations to leave. General Sullivan, the white warrior our men call the Blue Snake, comes closer to our people. Our people die at his hand. Our corn is trampled by his horses. He leaves no blade of grass in his path."

"He is so near?"

"We have heard the big gun at each new sun and the rising of the night lights. Our village is large. We are his prey."

Mary instinctively held Jesse close to her to shelter him from danger. The council fires had spoken of this General as the sword of Washington. This was a white man's war, over the land of the Indians. The Seneca called it the Whirlwind, the white men who passed through the village called it the Revolution.

"Sister, where will we make our stand?"

"We will not stand. It is a sad day for our nation. We must huddle as children at the fort of the Red Jackets, near the thunder water of the Niagawa."

"Hiokatoo will fight?"

"He will not return for many seasons. He is in command of our warriors. His battles are many."

Mary watched as her sister walked away. She felt her sadness, her loss of dignity. She walked as a fallen hawk whose wings had been broken in flight, seeming desperate and useless.

Tom looked at her as he continued carving his totem, waiting for her signal, her command.

"War is not your way, my son. You are too gentle."

She cradled Jesse in her arms and smiled at his happy blue eyes.

"Your brother Jesse has a soft face, a farmer's eyes. War will not be his."

John rose and faced her defiantly.

"I will not go and hide with women and children. I will stand and fight, with my father. I am not afraid."

"The men go, too, John. We will not wait for the sound of Sullivan's horses. We will leave with the others."

She saw the frustration in John's eyes, but Hiokatoo had not ordered his children to battle. She gathered her things and hurried to the village. Tom pushed by John calling him a witch. Witchcraft was the greatest insult to a Seneca. When one was accused and proven to be a witch, that one was immediately killed so as not to undermine or upset the great Creator. Mary didn't understand her one son's accusation of another, especially coming from Tom. He was known as a gentle, caring boy, with no inclination toward violence.

She called both of them to her and sat them on either side facing away so as not to stir any anger.

"My sons, you are the blood of the Seneca nation. You are the body of a great people. What is this sickness between you? This evil that divides you?"

"My brother is not a Seneca. Our father does not accept him so I will not accept him."

Mary kept her silence at John's words. It was time for them to talk.

"And my brother is a witch. He kills deer when no others can and smiles at the blood on his hands."

"You can not hunt because you are like a woman!"

John tried to turn to Tom, but Mary turned him back. She felt the seething within them and her own heart cried to be mended. She took each of their hands in hers.

"John, you must not judge another by who accepts him. I, too, am not accepted by Hiokatoo, but I am Seneca. And as for hunting, it was me, dear son, who gave you your first tomahawk. It was me during your father's absence who taught you to track and find deer and elk and beaver. It was me who showed you the way to tire a bear for the kill. If Tom hunts like a woman, then he hunts like his mother, as you do."

She clenched John's hand to try to show him her love, then turned to Tom.

"And as for witches, my son. I, too, was called a witch by many who now call you brother. Because I could teach your brother to hunt, to hunt better than many others, I was threatened with a witch's death."

She took their hands and touched them together. Then, with a strength her sons had forgotten or never knew, she locked her arms around their necks and pulled them to her feet. Neither could struggle from her grasp.

"You are my sons and I intend to keep you."

With that she jerked them back to the ground and they sat in amazement and love of this woman they called mother.

Mary and her family joined her people at Fort Niagawa. It was a dismal scene. The warriors huddled in small circles, keeping their distance from the British. The British, the Red Jackets, expected favors from the Indian women and looked down on the mighty Seneca men.

Mary pounded samp and ground corn for the soldiers. The Seneca had wanted to stay neutral, and the colonists had also wanted their neutrality, but the British needed the Seneca strength, and the power of the other tribes who made up the Six Nations.

As Mary ground corn, A British soldier motioned for her

to come to him. She hurried to accommodate, carrying food with her to satisfy him.

"No, no. I feel quite full. It's the dampness I suffer from. From the mist. Could I trouble you for a blanket? Or some kind of cover to block the chill?"

Mary nodded and scurried back to her area for a blanket. She had only hers to give, but she gave it willingly.

"Thank you very much, Ma'am. So it's true. You're the captive I've heard of. I could tell it by your hair. How long have you been with them?"

Mary said nothing. She didn't consider herself a captive any longer. She could have returned to the white nation instead of going to her sisters, but she had chosen the kindness of the Seneca. The soldier continued.

"You know, of course, when this is over, we'll be asking the Indians for your freedom. Seems fair to us, I suppose. Don't know if the colonists would do the same if they happened to win. What do you think of that? Would you like your freedom?"

Mary looked at him with a Seneca pride some Indians would envy.

"Freedom is already mine to hold. No Red Jacket can give me this."

Another group waved her over to them. She met the soldier's eyes once more and left him. She could hear his laughter as she made her way across the open compound.

That night, as many slept, Mary went to speak to her sisters.

"It is safe now sisters. I have served many Red Jackets today who were near our village. They say Sullivan came. He found no one and retreated. They also say he burned the houses, and the corn. But he will not return. His mission is done. Washington has called him back."

The first sister sat dejected. Mary saw her as she had seen her father. Her will to survive was gone, her lifeblood dried from the scorching news of loss.

"We will not return. We will go to our old village and try to rebuild. We will await the word of our chiefs."

Mary was resolute. "I will not. I will go home, near the Gardeau, and await Hiokatoo."

"There is no shelter," the second sister said.

"I have strong sons who need work to rid them of their anger. We will make our way."

The sisters knew she meant what she said. Each rose and hugged her warmly. When the second sister hugged her she looked at Mary's eyes. Mary looked back, not sure whether she should tell them what else she had heard.

"What is it, Dehewamus? What else troubles you?"

"The soldiers spoke of their folly with our people. They told of the chiefs signing a paper, a treaty to keep them neutral in the white man's war. And then the Red Jackets told our warriors to go to a battlefield and watch the might of the Creator across the ocean. The British fed our men their spirits, the rum from barrels on their ships, then lined them up in front, as if they would be watching the women's dance at our fire. They could not watch. The colonists saw them as the beginning of the battle line. They were forced to fight for their lives! Many of our men were killed. The cry of revenge will echo through our Nation."

The first sister squeezed her hand and pulled Mary closer to her. "I fear for you, Dehewamus. There is a story you do not know and that story will be repeated soon. The great carrying place, the Niagawa, will see many die in the hole of the white man's devil. Our warriors once did this to the British and none lived. If you travel this path death may find you."

"I will travel my path to my husband." She kissed her sisters and left at the new sun.

PART III

8

The forest was bare, empty of everything that wasn't forever green. Mary could hear scurrying chipmunks as they rushed to save their winter store. With two children on her back, nine year old John beside her, and Tom astride a horse in front, Mary inched her way through the lonely forest. It was almost too empty. She hadn't remembered it ever seeming so barren, so absolutely clean of leaves or dead branches. She wondered if wars did such things. She knew the death and desolation of war as far as people were concerned, but she never thought of its absolute destruction of the earth. Did her Seneca brothers know? Did they understand that killing people often meant killing land? They had killed other Indians in the Cherokee wars. Hiokatoo had commanded that destruction, that utter annihilation of a people. The Creator frowned on that, she was sure. The poor harvests and killing winters were their just punishment for such acts.

But now war was even more deadly. The balls from the big guns ripped through the trees, tearing limbs and sometimes blasting the very roots. She wondered about the animals who lived beneath the forest's cover. Were they too victims, left for dead by an enemy? She didn't like war. It was a man's game; a game of chance and hate and senseless duty. What pride could there be in victory over a fellow human? In the death of a brother or sister? The murder of a mother or father? A daughter or son? Why would men who loved their

Creator beyond definition want to destroy all the Creator gave them?

She jumped and laughed silently at her fear as a family of sparrows rushed from the fir beside her. In the distance she could hear the faint roar, the magnificent power of the falls. Tom turned to question the sound.

"Niagawa," said Mary. "Thunder Waters."

She kept a watchful eye, concerned about the flight of the birds, aware of a presence that meant to keep itself hidden. The sound of the water grew louder. She had never seen it, only heard of it described at council fires.

The men said it was the center of the Creator's world, a place where all life began and all life ended. They spoke of its mighty waters crashing to the pointed rocks below; Water so powerful it seemed to fly from the crest of the rapids and soar through the sky to its death. But it didn't die, they said. It landed with a thunderous crash and drew more life from its fate. It swirled and drew in its breath, sucking energy from all around it. In winter the mighty waters froze, holding their breath above the crevices and caves.

Tom's horse was frightened and stopped. With prodding Tom made him walk again and Mary was more watchful. WHOOSH! A deer darted from some scant brush, leaping away, its white tail bobbing right and left. John readied his knife and poised himself to run.

"Do not follow, my son. Our journey is long and we have only begun. There will be food."

She felt she should have let him chase it. If the woods were not fruitful on their journey they would go hungry. But they weren't hungry now, and the deer was provided for hunger and beauty. It was beauty's turn to triumph.

John grumbled at her decision, but he obeyed her as a son should. He was a natural warrior. From his birth Mary saw an anger, a distrust in his eyes that made him different from her other sons. He was Hiokatoo's son. Hiokatoo, a man who would lay down his life for a friend or brother. A man who would smash an infant's head against a rock if it was white or Cherokee.

A hand touched her shoulder, but she didn't cry out. She turned to face her husband. Hiokatoo made a covering motion on his mouth telling Mary to stay silent then took the reins from Tom and led his family deeper into the forest. A small band of Seneca waited in the clearing molding weapons and preparing for their next battle. Hiokatoo stopped the horse and pointed to Tom to sit on the ground. He then put an arm around John and began speaking to him about the war. Mary silently dropped her burden to the ground and dug roots for the children to chew to ensure their silence. Hiokatoo came to her.

"We are far enough. The white man's ears are not so strong. They will not hear us above the thunder water."

"Are we hunted, my husband?"

"We hunt. The white man brings a large army with wagons, horses. They were with Sullivan, The Blue Snake. We will wait for a sign from our Creator and they will pay with their lives."

"I must leave then. With the children."

"Our Red Jackets knew of your movement. You must stay until our mission is done."

He gathered Tom and John to him.

"You young ones will join us. Though we have many more numbers than the white man, you will be useful."

Tom looked to his mother for approval. Hiokatoo turned him to face him.

"Do not look to your mother on this subject, Tom. Women have no law with war. Come, I will show you the numbers we follow."

They climbed the high choppy cliffs overlooking the river. The sound of the falls was deafening, forcing their silence. Hiokatoo pointed to a narrow ridge that followed the gorge. The trail was loose and rocky. From their vantage point they could see the beginning of a long line of white men dressed in rags of various colors. Some walked. Some rode horses. They struggled with carts and wagons. All carried guns. Their path was winding and jagged. Their view was a treacherous drop of six hundred feet into a thunderous, grinding current.

Tom eyed two particular men who seemed somehow familiar to him. Their hair resembled his hair, their faces were similar to his reflection in the river. They rode with the columns, sometimes by twos, sometimes in single file to avoid a deadly fall. The first man looked determined in his ride. The man with him seemed unhappy, unable to maneuver as well as the first.

He was Mary's brother, John, now eighteen years older, leading his younger brother Jesse through a winding turn.

"Just try to keep the horse steady," John said. "Don't let 'er know you're scared. She'll feel it."

Jesse tried to avoid his brother's eyes.

"Never liked this idea in the first place, John. Why can't we just find us some land and get to farmin' like Pa would?"

"Watch that side!" John called out. "You go down and it'll be a six or seven hundred foot drop." He leaned to look over the edge. "Won't be no easy fall, either. Even it you make it to the water the current will chop ya to pieces!"

John's alarm made Jesse more nervous in his ride.

"I've been meanin' what I say, John. I'm a farmer, not a soldier."

John guided him a few more feet until he was on slightly safer ground.

"I'll make a deal with you, brother," John said. "You get at least one Indian this time. Just one. To avenge the death of your family. Get just one, and I'll consider quittin' and going back to farming."

Jesse shook his head as they continued to ride and maneuver.

"I just ain't got your hate, John"

"May be. But I don't wanna be shamed by you no more.

When men around you are fightin' for their lives, you be duty bound to fight back!"

Hiokatoo studied the movement of the army. He guessed their numbers to be three hundred.

Tom watched only John and Jesse, the uncles he never knew.

Hiokatoo looked at both his sons, then spoke to John.

"Our Creator has given us a signal. The army from Sullivan is tired and unsure of their path. We must hurry."

Hiokatoo rushed back to the clearing and gathered his weapons and men. He commanded his troops to the top of the gorge and sent messengers to signal the others. His forces were twelve hundred strong and this battle of revenge churned his blood.

"Your sons will be brave, Dehewamus."

"As will you, Hiokatoo."

She watched her husband and sons set off on their mission of destruction. As a wife of a warrior chief she was always ready for news of death. As a mother, never. John would survive, but her eldest was her strength. Though she found herself drawn more to Jesse now, for his loving manner, his youth, Tom was still her first-born, her symbol of motherhood.

The silent Seneca watched from the thick foliage of the hill. They hid themselves behind the oak and elm trees that surrounded the magnificent hole of death. On a signal from Hiokatoo, they descended, tomahawks raised, war whoops louder than the thundering rapids.

The horses and the men of the army below began immediately to fall into the gorge. They struggled to hold their horses steady, but no man's strength could overcome the fear of the war whoops. Men were thrown from their mounts over the edge, their bodies crashing and breaking against the rocks. The horses fell with them, on top of them, beside them. Carts and wagons rolled through the carnage.

Hiokatoo ruthlessly swung his tomahawk, his whip. He smiled at his work and his mission. Tom watched this father of his who showed him no love. He wanted to please him, to be accepted by him. He watched and copied, swinging, whooping, pushing men and horses over the edge. Trees descending the gorge crashed to the ground as the weight of wagons and men destroyed them. The army fired shots when they could, but the guns were unaimed, the attempt to attack futile.

Hiokatoo watched his son John grab the reins of a soldier and strike at his leg with a tomahawk. The soldier struggled with the horse and kicked at John. The horse fell from under him. The harness was broken and caught on a tree, saving the man from a further fall. The wounded soldier held on, gripping the harness with all his strength as he dangled over the gorge. John watched for a moment, then, smiling as his father, slammed the tomahawk against the leather. The snap of the harness ended the soldier's chances of survival. Hiokatoo watched as John eyed his tomahawk lovingly. He was pleased with his son.

Mary's brother John fell from his horse and held the reins. The horse slid further down the rocks, screaming for its life, struggling with all its power and might to stay alive. John held on, but the horse was too heavy. Before he, too, followed the horse over the edge he let go, screaming for his brother.

"Jesse! Jesse! Where are ya?"

Another man and his horse fell beside him. John was frightened as he watched them fall into the gorge. The man's body was twisted and broken, pieces of it sprayed the rocks with blood. John tried to climb up, away from the gore, but his leg was hurt, broken from his fall. He pulled and crawled into the trees. He grabbed limbs and strained to pull himself forward.

Tom watched his struggle. Though the man was familiar to him, he was also white. He knew Hiokatoo was watching. He chased through the trees after Mary's brother.

John dragged his battered leg behind him. He was far enough away from the drop to the gorge to feel safe. He reached up to another limb and pulled some more. His eyes froze on the tomahawk that sliced into the tree just above his hand. He turned to face Tom.

"But . . . you're white," he said.

Another tomahawk from the opposite direction sliced down into his brain. Tom jumped back from the splatter of blood and looked at the attacker, his brother.

"But I am Seneca," said John.

Mary, Jesse and baby Nancy waited in the clearing for the end of the battle. Jesse covered his ears to block the noise and Mary gently lowered his hands.

"There is no need to cover your ears, my son. Listen, instead, to what is in your heart."

She pulled Nancy closer to her. She heard the agony around them. She felt their terror.

"I will tell you a story of a Nation of the Niagawa. A nation that, in each new season of warmth, chose a maiden from among them. A maiden of the forest to please the spirit of the Thunder Water. The maiden was placed in a canoe filled with flowers of the new sun and fruits of the season.

"One spring, the beautiful maiden, the daughter of a famous chief, was chosen to appease the water. The father hid his heartbreak, as he was an Indian, and the canoe, guided by the maiden, swept out into the swift current of the great falls.

"Just as it did, another canoe shot swiftly from a different bank and closely followed the maiden's canoe to its death. It was the chief, the maiden's father.

"The chief was well loved by his people and, so, the maiden was the last to be sacrificed. The chief and his daughter still dwell in a crystal cave under the great falls in the mist."

Mary knew the legend was a white man's version, but she

was unfamiliar with the legend of the Thunder Gods and was more concerned with comforting her children.

* * *

The Seneca lined the banks of the gorge to look for survivors. Debris was everywhere. Blood dotted the rocks and trees. Bodies still crashed through the rapids, disappearing under the water. The Seneca had won this battle. One man, only one, was still alive. His broken body sat precariously on a small ledge, half-way down the gorge wall. The Seneca watched him struggle to move. They appreciated strength and courage. The man's legs were nearly torn from their sockets. His blood dripped rhythmically to the rocks below. He was left to die in the hole of death.

Mary heard only the roar of the falls now. The war whoops had ended. The screams and shrieks were gone. She knew the mission was complete. She felt a heaviness in her heart. Her sons had gone to battle and not yet returned. She was afraid that death would visit her once again and she couldn't bear any more. There was also a new feeling inside her, one she couldn't explain. A different heaviness that left her empty and cold. She waited and waited, rocking her baby. At last Hiokatoo appeared. He looked older to Mary. She knew the years of battle were finally starting to erode his youth. He didn't smile. In fact, he wore no expression at all. Mary searched his eyes, his walk, for a sign about the fate of her sons, but he gave away nothing. He sat away from her, drained and worn as she continued to watch his face.

At last she saw the glimmer of a smile as he looked at his son. John came to him proudly, his tomahawk still covered with blood. Mary welcomed him, but he was more intent on preening for his father. She searched beyond him for her other son. Tom walked to her limply. His tomahawk hung from his hand, freshly cleaned. This son was not proud. He stopped at John's prideful glare, then walked past his family to his horse.

Mary felt his shame, but also was grateful this son was not a warrior.

"Jesse, tend your sister. Your brother is in need of a strong hand."

She went first to John who shied away from her touch in the company of other men.

"You are worthy of your pride, my John. Your war-pole will show your bravery and your children will know you as a killer of men."

She met her husband's eyes and nodded respect for his triumph. Then she cautiously walked to the son of Sheninjee.

His back was to her and she dared not touch him for fear of awakening a remorse or a tear that a mother's touch can often do.

"You have done well, my son. Your father's pride will show in the respect others give you. You will lead us back to our home, as I trust you more than any other."

Tom almost turned to her, then stopped at John's glare. He mounted his horse and waited for his mother's command.

9

Mary and her children approached their old village as a different family now. Her sons had seen their first battle and were suddenly men, or thought themselves to be. There was a gentleness missing from their talk, a coolness about them that Mary didn't like.

The homes made of bark were burned to ashes. The fruit trees that had sustained them through many springs were chopped to the ground and crushed into the earth. The corn fields were burned and trampled. The precious corn. Sullivan's destruction had been complete.

"It is the white man's way," Mary said.

She searched carefully through the ashes of her longhouse. The blackened wood crunched beneath her feet as she spread the ashes with her moccasins until she found what she was looking for. She first saw the blackened hawk carved and painted in the oak wood. Its wings were burned, parts of them lost to ash. She slowly pulled what remained up through the ashes. The yellow corn tassels had been spared from the fire, but the bottom half of the board was gone. The cradle board from Sheninjee. She rubbed the wood with her hand until her fingers were as black as the charred bark, then she spread the blackness on her face and packed the board in her burden sack.

They checked the fruit trees for any fruit remaining, but the soldiers had destroyed or taken everything.

Mary was sad and panicked as she searched for direction.

She checked her provisions. The food supply was low. She couldn't go back. She didn't know what had happened since she left Niagawa. She didn't know if Sullivan had returned, if the British still held the fort, if the war was over. Like a trapped animal she paced from side to side. It was her choice now. Hiokatoo would be gone for many more seasons. He was not the same companion Sheninjee had been. Her sisters were alive or dead someplace else. Her people were scattered, their chosen place killed by Washington's sword. The blackness around her reminded her of Teddy and Calvin. She remembered Calvin's description of the great falls. The three tiers. The river that ran backwards. Her choice was made. She would follow the river to the Gardeau. There she would make her home.

They were tired and worn. Her sisters had told her the Gardeau was ten suns and moons away, but already they had walked much longer. Never again would she trek in search of a home. She was dispirited and weak. She craved love and stability and peace and warmth and kindness and life.

They reached an area of chestnut trees and searched the ground for acorns. John also searched for herbs, something he seemed good at doing. Mary wished he would follow the path of healing his people, rather than the destruction of others. They huddled beneath a tree and piled their findings so that all could equally share.

Fall foliage and the breadth of the canyon made a magnificent view for Mary and her family. The exposed rock of the gorge was shale and sandstone and the mighty river carved its way through twists and turns. It was lined on all sides by great towering oak trees, with silver maples and firs as companions.

The first falls was more than seventy feet high, tossing its water out from its crest. The second falls had a ledge of more than a hundred feet and its water tumbled even more to the third tier. The gorge was lush with color and the mist from the falls rose into the sky. Mary could see a rainbow formed in the sun above the mist.

"It is our Creator's gift," she said. "He gives us the colors of the sky, the power of the water, the strength of the trees. Here we shall make our home."

Fruit trees stood in the distance and a great flat area overlooked the falls. Here Mary paced the dimensions of her house. She let her daughter hang from her cradle board watching the mist and the rainbow while she and her sons gathered bark and wood for her house.

They layered the bark and tied it with deer hide, strengthening the structure with fallen tree trunks. Mary carried the wood as always with her burden strap, down and around the rocky hillsides, across the stiller waters where the river narrowed.

They found other Seneca building and rebuilding a small village nearby. They hand plowed a large corn field to have it ready for spring and Mary made them clothes for winter from the hides that John and Tom supplied. She was happy here. She prayed each day for peace. Peace among white men. Peace among Indians. Peace between all men. And peace between her sons. Though they worked together to help her build, they hunted separately, shunning each other's company. Their eyes showed hatred and disgust. Tom was merciless. Each time John passed him he would call him a witch. Yet he was kind and loving to her. Though she didn't like or understand Tom's attitude toward his brother, it was John she worried about the most. His manner was always that of a warrior and she saw in him a way too much like Hiokatoo. She worried he could be as ruthless and cruel.

Jesse was constant. As he grew older he grew more serene. He avoided the company of other Indians, preferring the ways of the white men who travelled through the area. He helped her in the corn fields because there were no women to do the work. As Nancy grew older she took her place in the field, but Jesse was still there, providing for her in a way no man had ever done.

⬥⬥⬥ ⯐ ⬥⬥⬥

The corn field was showing its tassels as twelve year old Jesse made his way through the long stalks. Mary tended an outdoor fire on land that was now part of a larger Seneca village. Black Coals, the messenger of the tribe and a friend to Mary, advanced to her place near her longhouse.

"Dehewamus. The peace has been made."

"It is time for the Seneca to live in peace. I am happy for our people."

"My father, the Chief Sachem, wishes you to join his fire."

Mary tapped her lip and held back a smile.

"I hope, my brother, you mean for me to sit at his fire and not be burned within it."

She was the English teacher of her people and she often played with words to trick her Indian family. It was playful trickery, meant to ensure they knew the language of the white man, and knew it well enough to not be tricked or swindled in their trading.

Black Coals nodded and smiled. "Yes, yes. Again I have forgotten the 'at' word. At the fire, my sister. Please."

Though much older than he, Mary followed Black Coals' quick step to his father's fire.

Several chiefs sat next to a war-totem marked in red. Tomahawk grooves depicted battles and skins and scalps were the tales of victories. The Chief Sachem rose and took Mary's hand in greeting.

"Dehewamus, you are welcome at our fire."

She sat in the circle of men and the chief continued.

"I have news, my sister. The white nation has retreated. The great Seneca nation has agreed to peace."

Mary nodded. She knew the chief wasn't telling the whole truth. The Seneca had agreed to peace in their defeat. Hiokatoo had visited many times and spoke of the ruin of the nation. She was disappointed in the chief. She knew the Seneca lived in truth and guessed that their defeat had robbed the chief of his dignity. How sad it was that a nation so strong and enamored of truth must now stoop to a white man's game of lying.

"We have also agreed to release all those who have lived with us as Seneca. All whose blood comes from across the big water. You came to us many seasons ago, my sister. And you have served us well. Your house brings honor to our people. The Red Jackets speak proudly of your evening labor, pounding the samp and corn to provide them with food. And of your vigils under the moon, making clothes to protect them. We have agreed to your freedom, Dehewamus."

Mary stiffened at his words. What freedom did he mean? Did he think she had labored for the British so the colonists would make her free? Free of what? Of the beautiful valley she called home? Of the people around her she had grown to love and respect?

"But my home is here. You are my people. My family is of Iroquois blood, my children Seneca. I want no freedom from here."

"The white chiefs will pay a ransom for you."

"I will not be ransomed."

The chief's stern looked turned to a smile. She had worried he would make her go. The nation now needed money to sustain it. The white settlers were hunting and trading the hides of the Indians. They were taking land that bore fruit and other food once saved for the Nations.

"You honor us again, my sister. You are truly a Seneca. Because you honor us we have agreed to set your case before the great council of Big Tree. We will give you the land you have toiled on. You will pace it with Black Coals. The land you wish will be yours."

Mary was excited, but hesitated to show it so as not to seem greedy. She paused, bowed, and smiled at the chief.

"I know the land I wish. I will pace it. I am the one honored by you."

She walked the land with Black Coals. She crossed the river and paced there. She went into the gorge, up the rocky sides, down the bends and turns. She went into the forest and across fields of corn.

"Am I taking too much?" she asked Black Coals.

"You deserve it Dehewamus, but I caution you. The council chiefs can only deem what they wish you to have, but the land is now the land of Washington. It is his Generals who will decide your tract."

Whites and Seneca, chiefs and soldiers, suited men and settlers all gathered in a circle at Big Tree. Mary was the only woman. A large fire burned in the center. The council would stay and make all decisions until all agreed to put out the fire.

A tall, strong man dressed in buckskins approached Mary with his hand extended. Mary noticed a glint of mischief in his eye.

"Dehewamus? Ma'am, I'm Horatio Jones."

"Ah, yes. I have heard of you, Mr. Jones."

"Yes, Ma'am. I guess most have. I'm here to help you beat that old Red Jacket."

Though she didn't know who he meant, she looked at him with amusement. He carried his knife as a Seneca. A tomahawk was fashioned at his hip. Yet he was white, and here to help her beat a Seneca.

"What makes you believe I need help in my case, Mr. Jones?"

"Well, I've been around Red Jacket for some number of years. Do most of his interpreting when he won't use his English. You'd think he'd know by now that almost all the Indians know English. He ain't foolin' no one. And they don't call him Keeper Awake for nothin'. Why, I once saw him speak for two days. Every time someone started to fall asleep that old weasel would sneak up on 'em and pinch 'em right in the nose. Yep. He's somethin'. He's not ready to give away land. He thinks the whites are stealin' it."

"And are they, Mr. Jones?"

"Stealin? No Ma'am! They pay good money for land. Oh-oh. Looks like old Red Jacket's been hittin' the rum. Be lucky if we're done with business by the time the snow flies. He don't want you havin' any land and he's aimin' to make sure you don't get it."

Mary surveyed the large crowd. Among it she spotted a Seneca wearing a bright red British jacket. Around his neck was a large silver medal. Mary met his eyes. They were stern and cold. He teetered on his heels and swayed slightly as he moved through the crowd.

"Would this be Sagu-yu-what-heh? Keeper Awake?"

"Yep. The great O-rator himself."

"You know him well."

"Ha! I was a Seneca once, too. For fifteen years. Just like you I was with 'em. How long you been one?"

"I don't know as I remember, exactly. Forty summers. Maybe more."

Red Jacket stood at the front of the circle trying to silence the crowd.

"Friends? My friends? Listen to me with your ears. I speak to you today on the claim of Mrs. Mary Jemison. A claim for land only Seneca can call their own. The Seneca, Keepers of the Western Door of the Longhouse. Brothers to the Mohawk, Oneida, Onondaga, Cayuga, and Tuscarora. The white man promises the Seneca many things. The Seneca will always hunt the land, says he, no matter which white man holds the paper that claims it. This will not be so. The white man does not respect the land. He makes no attempt to share with his brothers. He does not speak with truth in his heart. He is not Seneca. Mary Jemison is not Seneca!"

The crowd murmured against him. Mary was hurt by his words. It hurt her that a man who didn't know her could judge her. Judge her blood. She also remembered her family. Her white family. Her father had laid claim to his land and shared only his table and his beliefs. It was true. She was Tom Jemison's daughter. He was a white man. Did this make her white? Why was it always color that decided one's fate?

"Hear me! A Seneca will not deed land to a white woman!"

The crowd grew angrier. Mary couldn't tell where their anger was directed. She didn't want to be suddenly hated because of a whiteness she had long forgotten. Horatio Jones jumped forward and stood next to Red Jacket.

"Wait! Red Jacket speaks some truth. Mary Jemison was once a white girl. A young girl from what is now called Pennsylvania, from the other side of the demarcation line."

Red Jacket seemed pleased with Jones and nodded for him to continue.

"But, today, and for many days past, she has lived as a Seneca!"

"No matter! Her blood is white!" Red Jacket seethed. He went to the fire and tried to kick the dirt to douse it, a signal that the council was over. Jones grabbed him and pulled him back.

"But the blood she has shed in bearing her children is Seneca. The blood of her husband when wounded in battle is Seneca. This deed is not given by the Seneca. It is the white nation who owns rights to this land now. They are giving back to a Seneca by giving it to Mrs. Jemison. For this, Red Jacket, you should be glad. As a Seneca, a great chief who will long be remembered for your words, you should be pleased that one of your people will retain rights to this land. She will stay with her people, the Seneca. Her houses will remain standing. Her fields will continue to bear corn. . . ."

113

A tear streaked Mary's face as she watched and listened, but she stood tall, with a serene and noble look. Into the evening they argued and debated until Mary could no longer stand silent. Regally she joined Jones and Red Jacket. The crowd murmured and hushed. No woman had ever spoken at a council fire.

"Oh men of the great Seneca Nation," she began. "You give pride to the Great Creator in all your deeds. The women of your tribe have respected you. My husband, Hiokatoo, has spoken of you with a father's pride. My children look up to you and know it is in you that they find truth and life. My children are Seneca. Will you deny them the fruits of the valley? The corn of our sustenance? Are my sons to live as white men, to be scorned and ridiculed as liars because they are truly Indian?"

She turned her gaze to Red Jacket.

"Saguyuwhatheh. You wear the coat of an English man. Yet you are a Seneca chief. You bear the medal of a white chief. Yet you are a speaker for your people. If I am not a Seneca, what then are you?"

Red Jacket cherished the coat given him by the British. He wore the medal from Washington with pride and conceit. Mary knew she had beaten him, but she didn't want him humbled before white men.

"Red Jacket. Let us be Seneca together, as our ways and our memories tell us to. Because you are a Seneca, I will accept your word."

Red Jacket straightened with renewed pride. Glancing at her sideways, he raised his hand to the crowd as a King over his subjects.

"I have heard the arguments of Mr. Jones, and of the White Woman of the beautiful valley. The great Hiokatoo, Gardeau, is her husband. If the council agrees, I will not block it. The land by the great river shall be hers, forever named the Gardeau Tract."

Jones gave Red Jacket a hard slap on his back, almost

knocking him over, and shook his hand in gratitude. The crowd nodded their approval and went on to consider the next case. Jones smiled ear-to-ear at the woman he'd grown close to so quickly.

"Mary. Mrs. Jemison, you have your land. But you still have to present your boundaries to Mr. Parrish. Beware. He isn't willing to give up much of the beautiful valley."

Jones led Mary away from the circle to the longhouse that officed Mr. Parrish. As they entered they saw Mr. Parrish sitting at a make-shift table strewn with papers. He was asleep on one arm. Jones sneaked up close to him and slammed his hand on the table. Mr. Parrish knocked his papers to the floor and then fell down on top of them. Mary and Jones stood stoically watching. When Parrish regained his composure he looked at Mary and sneered, then directed his gaze at Jones.

"This is the woman with the land? The one who'll present her boundaries?"

Jones just smiled silently. Mary was amused that Parrish spoke only to Jones, ignoring her presence as a woman. She also waited silently.

"Did you hear me, man?"

"He heard," Mary said.

Parrish looked at Mary, surprised.

"You speak English? I thought you were an Indian!"

"Both are true."

"Well, are you the one?"

"I am."

"Do ya know your boundaries?"

"I do."

"Good. Can you state them for me?"

"I can not."

Parrish looked at her disgruntled. He glanced at Jones and saw his smile but no attempt to help. Mary finally eased his confusion.

"I do not know the terms you use. I only know the pacing I have done with my brother."

"Pacing? Well, can you tell me the number of chains and links?"

"I can not. What I can tell you is a large forest stands to one side, and my corn field bounds the other. I can view the falls, and I can follow the river. I can look back and see the sun as it rises. Those are my boundaries."

While Mary spoke Parrish looked at his maps and charts trying to determine where she meant. Frustrated he looked up at her with a furrowed brow.

"How old are you?"

"I have lived almost fifty-five winters."

"Winters? You mean years? Well, how much land can a woman of fifty-five possibly use?"

He pulled out some papers and made some marks on them. He drew lines while Mary pointed, almost drawing him a map with her hands. At last he sighed with relief.

"Okay. Put your mark here. And I'll put mine with the seal of Washington. And we'll be done with it."

Both parties made their marks and Mary smiled graciously at Parrish. She had her land. She would build houses for her children and keep them forever near her. She would sustain her people with the corn from her fields. Parrish waved her away, disgusted, and she and Jones left. Jones put his arm around her shoulder and laughed.

"Mrs. Jemison. Mary. That was the best piece of schemin' I ever did see. Do you know how much land Mr. Parrish just signed away to you?"

"I believe in your terms, Mr. Jones, it works out to eighteen thousand acres. Or so my son Tom says."

10

Mary and Tom walked through their corn fields together. He was thirty-two and, though he dressed in some Seneca and some white clothing, in Mary's eyes he had grown more handsome. Her fields had also grown and Mary saw them as a tremendous amount of work that she could no longer handle. She kept her hand on Tom's shoulder, more for affection than support, and she loved the way he straightened when she touched him.

"The people who will share our crops will come soon. It's not kind to the Earth leaving it unattended to go to weed."

Tom was hurt by her words and she felt his shoulders slump under her touch. She knew his hurt came from shame. He was always the conflicted one. A part of him so much wanted to be Seneca. Another part couldn't help being white. He wanted to help her in the fields as Jesse did, but he feared Hiokatoo's indignation.

"My son, you hide your eyes like a child. I have depended on you always, and loved you for your kindness and strength. But the winds push me closer to my end and the land grows stronger with each new sun. Mr. Parrish has told me I can lease my land and share in its gathering. It is time."

Tom studied her face and nodded. Mary still saw her father in his eyes. Even when he was troubled his eyes twinkled when he looked at her.

John ran to them dressed, as usual, in full Seneca clothing.

117

This was the Indian in Mary's life. He never touched her. Never came close enough to her for her to feel his love.

"Come with me, brother Tom. The men join in games of strength. Seneca games."

"I choose to stay here."

"Because you are afraid? Because you crave your mother's dress?"

Tom's rage grew quickly. Mary felt his shoulder tighten and coil to strike. She firmed her touch to hold him back. Coolly and calmly he answered.

"I don't like the company of witches."

Now John's rage took over. Mary took her hand from Tom's shoulder.

"Why do you call me a witch? Since you were small I have been a witch to you. The Seneca penalty for this is death."

He raised his tomahawk in challenge to Tom.

"Do you wish to try to kill me?"

Mary moved her body between them as they stared at each other with hatred.

"I am not like you, brother John. I do not kill as a game."

Mary looked at each and motioned for them to leave in different directions. They parted sourly, but always obeyed her. She watched to be sure they both walked their distance then turned and smiled when she saw Horatio Jones riding up on his horse. She sighed to clear the pain her sons caused in her heart.

"Mr. Jones! You've come for one of my special cakes?"

Jones looked pleased to see her and she loved his smile.

"Could be, if you're makin' em!"

"I would make them special, if it is to your liking."

Mary glanced once again at her sons, to be sure of their paths.

"Those two still havin' trouble seeing eye to eye?"

"Since they were babies cutting their teeth on bark. Tom believes his brother to be a witch, for reasons I have never known. He also judges him for holding two women in his house. Two wives are accepted by our council, but not by my son Tom."

"Looked like they were comin' to blows."

"Let it not worry you, Mr. Jones. Tom is a gentle warrior. And John is a true Seneca, son of his father. John will not strike unless in defense. And, as long as the spirits of the white man, the rum and the whiskey, do not reach Tom's lips, there will be no battle."

"Speakin' of rum. Passed a whole wagon of it on my way here. Must be time for the fall frolic."

Mary was surprised. She had forgotten. The fall frolic was one of the five festivals of the year.

"It is true! I must prepare!"

She walked quickly away from Jones to the side of her house. There she uncovered a large wooden vat. She grasped the leather attached to it and fastened it as a burden strap on her forehead. Jones looked on with a smile. He had seen her do this before. Though the vat was heavy, three times her weight, she dragged it to a special circle drawn in red in front of her house. She entered the longhouse and quickly returned with a skin, a gun and a tomahawk. She placed the skin beside the vat and then leaned the weapons against it.

"Now, the men of our village will see. And remember. Come, Mr.Jones. I will give you your cake."

Inside the longhouse lay Hiokatoo. He was much older and very sick. His skins were on the side bench, on the side closest to the fire. He looked at Jones in recognition, but didn't move or speak. Jones nodded to him with respect as Mary placed a small cake in Jones' hand.

"My husband has suffered many seasons with the white man's disease."

"It's called consumption. Been killin' off many of the settlers."

"Are there many who now come, Mr. Jones?

He nodded his head and chewed on his cake.

"Yep. Seems like there's more wagons every day. The old paths look like rivers."

Hiokatoo coughed, and then choked. Mary had heard it often, but this seemed worse. He stretched his wrinkled and knotted hand toward Mary. Their eyes met and she nodded knowingly. From a holder on the wall above him she took down his tomahawk. It looked as old and worn as his hands. She fixed a piece of deer hide that had come loose then carefully handed it to him. He didn't take his eyes off her as he gripped his tomahawk with the last of his strength. Mary spoke to him softly.

"Your journey will be a good one, Hiokatoo. You have pleased the Great Creator."

Hiokatoo rested the tomahawk on his chest, closed his eyes, and died. Jones watched Mary as she calmly took ashes from the fire and smeared them on her door.

"I'll tell the others," said Jones.

"His burial will be in two suns. He will have all dignity as he follows his path."

At dusk the loud sounds of the frolic began. A lonely Mary sat on the skin near the vat. In the distance there was whooping and hollers near the large fire of the fall festival. Warriors came to her vat as she sat staring. They deposited their weapons in a pile—knives, tomahawks, powder bags, flints, clubs. Some were reluctant as they looked at the old woman, but they complied with respect. Mary looked at no one. She maintained this silent vigil during every frolic. She felt she needed to stop her people from self-destruction. She knew the powers of alcohol. She remembered the changes in her father and she knew stories of death that followed those changes.

Behind her, through the open door of the longhouse, revealed by the flickering fires, lay the body of Hiokatoo. This was her husband of more than forty years.

With him she had borne six children. But Mary didn't miss him. She knew his life would be missed by the Seneca. By the Six Nations. He had commanded seven campaigns against both Indians and whites. She respected him for never insulting her or treating her with less respect than was due a warrior's wife. But she didn't miss him.

Tom came near, carrying a gun and a knife. She could see he had already been drinking and she looked at him in anger. He threw his weapons in the vat, but did it in such a way that she felt offended by him.

"Your weapons should have been the first, my son, before your lips touched the evil spirits of the white man."

"It was good. And it was there. Couldn't wait. At least I got here."

"You will be the first to be bound on this night, Tom. And the first I will see with the new sun."

He sneered at her and stuck his hands in his white man's pockets. Balancing on one foot, he peered through the open door at Hiokatoo and raised his hand in a wave.

"May your trip be a happy one. . . ."

Then, under his breath, "You old Indian."

He left for the frolic and Mary sighed to contain her anger.

Soon John came, also carrying weapons. Mary noticed he was very sober. He nodded to his mother as he came closer and softly put his weapons in the vat. Then he entered the longhouse to solemnly sit with his father. Mary watched as he knelt by Hiokatoo and quietly wept. She turned away so as not to embarrass him.

Next it was Horatio Jones who came to her. Jones and John nodded at each other as John left toward the forest. Jones took his gun and his long knife and placed it on the pile.

"Well, Mary. How many will there be tonight?"

Mary shook her head in disgust.

"More than the corn in my fields. My Tom will be the first one bound."

"Well, could be lucky for Tom. First one drunk, first one bound, first one to sleep it off. He'll be up with the sun."

He left the old woman to her quiet vigil.

Mary stayed her post through the night. At dawn, as the sun rose over the gorge she loved, she decided her task was complete. She replaced her weapons and skin in her house, then started her obligatory walk through the village.

She slowly searched for her sons among the bound men. It was a practice for sober men to tie the hands of those who drank. Their hands were then tied to their feet, preventing them from walking or striking out at each other in their drunkenness. Mary was always the guard of the weapons. She felt it necessary to avoid any accidents. She was outspoken and determined about the effects of alcohol on the Indians. She tried to tell them it was against their nature, against the will of the Creator. But the Indians were changing. To her each day was a war that they lost. Each day they learned something new from the white man. Something new and destructive.

Some of the bound men moaned in their sleep, others were still completely unconscious. Mary walked and searched. There were literally hundreds of bound Seneca before her. The sight disgusted her. And saddened her.

There was Tom, sleeping and boyish. To her he seemed babyish. The slight smile on his face and the fetal pose made all her maternal instincts rise to the surface. She knelt next to him, then sat, making a lap of her ever strong legs. Gently she rolled him to her until she had rolled him onto her lap. Then, as she had done so often when he was a baby, she rocked him and rocked him in her arms. She quietly whispered to him.

"My son, my son. I will love you forever. I will always be your mother. You will always be my son."

She rocked him some more, as only a mother can, and she saw his smile grow wider in his sleep.

Jesse joined her, dressed as a white man. She knew he was fine because he shunned frolics, refused to go.

"Found him, huh? Where's John?"

Mary shook her head. She didn't know.

"I haven't seen him, either. Could be in the forest, gathering more herbs. He didn't get as drunk as the others last night. Guess Tom had him too riled, callin' him a witch again."

Mary looked back at Tom and rocked him some more.

"I'll get to work in the fields. Just want to see Hiokatoo for awhile."

Mary looked up at him lovingly. Though she held her first born in her arms, Jesse was still her favorite and it showed in her eyes.

The next day Mary dressed Hiokatoo in his finest Seneca garb. Beside him and around him she carefully placed his implements of war. She polished his tomahawk and knife and put them near his hands. His powder flask and flint went beside him. A cup was placed near his head in case he thirsted on his journey. As a final gesture, she placed a small cake still warm from the ashes near the head of the man she called husband. She smiled at her companion and moved away. Some Seneca men lifted the skin he lay on and gently placed him in a grave. The site was in Mary's private cemetery, reserved for all members of her family. Another skin was placed on top, and then some more to warm him on his way.

11

A white man and his Seneca wife worked in one of Mary's fields. She showed them how to plant the corn and work the soil to ensure the best crop. They were grateful and friendly as she parted with them and went to her house. Jones waited at her door, the usual smile on his still-handsome face.

"How are they working?"

"They know the corn. My sharecroppers now number five families."

"Got room for any more?"

Mary looked at him questioningly.

"Met a man the other day who swears he's a cousin of yours. Calls himself George Jemison."

Mary tried to remember.

"George Jemison? George? George . . ."

"Says he was comin' round to see you when the raidin' party came."

"Ah, yes. Cousin George. A scoundrel, or so my father told us. I never met him. Not that I remember. But my brother John spoke often of his hatred for him."

"Don't know if he's a scoundrel or not. Why, the man is rag-poor. Got him a young wife and two children. He's near about your age, probably more. Well, we got to talkin' and when I told him I knew a Jemison name of Mary, his eyes lit up like a fire at a frolic. Told him to come and see you. Told him maybe he could share-crop here."

124

Mary wasn't sure she wanted someone so detested by her family to share any of what was hers.

"I will ask the advice of Black Coals on this matter."

"Already have. Cornplanter and Black Coals think it's an honor to have one of your family join you. They say it's the Seneca way."

"Cornplanter was my husband's brother. Black Coals has been my friend and counsel. George Jemison is not my family, Mr. Jones. My family is Seneca. But it is the Seneca way to help one who calls himself family. Let it be so."

Mary opened her door to a worn and haggard man, his hat in hand, his clothes torn and dirty.

"Why, Mary, Lass! It truly be you!"

Mary forced a smile. "And you are George. George Jemison."

"That I be! Cousin to your father's brother, rest Tom's soul. And you be Tom's daughter. Last time I saw ya, you was but a wee thing."

"Do you wish food after your journey?"

"Aye. My family is hungry. In need of a place to stay."

"My houses are open to all who enter. My food is their food."

"You sound a little like old Tom himself."

Mary dropped her eyes and sighed. The mention of her father still brought tears. Still an uncontrollable sadness.

"Oh, I'm sorry, Lass. For a moment . . . well, you know. Your brothers and I searched for ya. High and low. 'Til we came to the fires. Why, we thought you were among 'em. Killed with the rest."

Mary's eyes brightened at the mention of her brothers. Excitement filled her at the thought of them still being alive. She wondered if God had brought this stranger to her to re-unite her with her past.

"My brothers. They are alive?"

"No. No . . . no. Heard they joined up with a renegade bunch. Travelled with Washington, they did. Got caught up in some trap. Up near Niagara. Devil's Hole, I believe they call it now. All twelve hundred of them, surrounded by Seneca."

He shook his head, marvelling at the thought.

"Right over they went, splashing into the gorge."

"You are sure my brothers were there?"

"Aye, Mary. They hated the Indians . . . I mean, sorry. That be their words. Hateful of what happened to their family. It ate at them. Bein' the Irish lads they were, Irish, same as you, they stood ready to fight. John much more than Jesse, but, still. I tried to keep track of 'em. See if they went back to the farm or not. Then I heard they went over that gorge."

Mary now knew why she had felt so heartsick at the Niagawa. If only her brothers had kept running. If only they had stayed farmers and not fighters. It was far too late for 'if onlys'.

"Well," George said. "I'll be gettin' my family, then. Got me a pretty young wife. And two boys from her dead husband. Killed in the Revolution, you know? There'll be work?"

Mary was composed, in control. Thoughtful of all George had said.

"You and your family can work the north fields. In English terms it is forty acres or so."

George put his hat back on, brushed off his clothes, then tipped his hat at Mary as he left.

"We're thankful to you, Mary. And thankful to the Lord you're still alive."

As he parted her a Seneca raced across the fields toward her. He passed George who shied away from him in fear.

"Dehewamus! You must come quickly!"

Mary nodded and followed him, still as quick in her step as the young warrior. She followed him through the gorge to a clearing and a small bark house. A crowd of Seneca women and men surrounded it. Mary was unsure what to expect as she searched the faces of the crowd for a sign. The warrior pushed people aside to let Mary pass.

There on the ground lay Tom's body, stabbed and bleeding.

Mary grabbed herself as if to keep her insides from bursting out. She tried with all her might to hold back the sobs that quickly and completely overwhelmed her body. Her grief was too great. She wailed and threw herself on the bloody remains of her son. She didn't know where to touch. How to touch him. If she should touch him. Other women tried to pull her away, to hold her back. She fought them, wailing and screaming, searching the crowd for an answer.

"My Tom. My baby Tom! Who killed my son? Who killed my baby?"

She grabbed and shook those who would look at her. She needed to know. She threw aside each person who wouldn't answer. With the strength and power of a mad woman she separated the crowd. Her hands shook and whitened in her rage. Her heart pounded against her throat, her chest, her very being.

"Who killed this son of my heart? This boy who looked like a man?"

She spun around, back to her son's body. Slowly she neared it, knelt beside it. Carefully she rolled him into her lap and rocked him. Back and forth. Back and forth. His blood dripped and mixed with her tears. Back and forth. Back and forth.

"My baby, Tom. I'll love you forever. Forever and always I'll be your mother. Forever and always you'll be my son. Forever and always. Forever and always."

Back and forth. Back and forth.

Black Coals came and sat beside her, careful to keep his distance, but close enough to be a friend.

"The old men say it was John. Tom drank the white man's spirits and did not hide his weapons. There was no one to bind him as he came for his brother. The old men say John was right and just in striking back, They have gone to a council fire in Buffalo to make their mark for John's freedom from punishment."

Warriors came and pulled Tom's body from her. She held

herself, cradling a missing baby. She knew the men didn't really believe John was just. He was Hiokatoo's son. They would shame Hiokatoo by punishing John. She shuddered as she realized she wanted John dead.

Jesse came to her slowly, not ashamed of the tears on his cheeks. He knelt in front of her and she could feel the awful pain in his eyes.

"Mama. My mother. My heart cries out for you."

Mary reached out to dry his tears, savoring the feel of his warm skin, the love that flowed from him.

"Do not cry, my Jesse. A Seneca man must never cry."

Jesse couldn't hold back. She watched his lips quiver and his body shake as he struggled to please her.

"I am not a Seneca. I am the son of my mother."

Mary smiled at him as well as she could and cupped his cheek in her hand. She knew he was right. He wasn't a Seneca. Not like Hiokatoo. Not like the warriors. But she also knew he wasn't white. He valued all around him. He would never waste a part of nature. He maintained a love and respect for her that was unequaled by any white man. White men killed for no reason and treated their brothers with envy. They took whatever they thought was theirs and took from others with no regret. This man before her was not white. He dressed as a white man and his manner of walking and speech were modelled after them, but he respected all people. He wasn't afraid to love them, to show his love. He didn't hold himself above anyone, nor would he compete just to win.

"My son, you are loved by your mother as no other can be loved. Because you are mine, you are Seneca."

Jesse hesitated, then fell forward into her arms. This was truly the son of her heart.

She buried Tom in her cemetery, but away from Hiokatoo. She gave him a funeral more like that of white men. He had never been a true warrior. She fixed a bark carving above his grave and visited every day. Today it rained. A drizzling constant rain that made it seem forever morning. Again her cousin George came with his hat in his hand.

"Mary, Lass. I'm needin' to talk with you about the land."

Mary was puzzled. For two years George and his family had worked the land. She had paid off his debts and bought him a cow. She clothed him and his family though she didn't have enough hides to make clothes for herself.

"Is the land not good? Two seasons of harvest have brought much corn to your family."

"Oh, it's fine. Just fine. But, I been talkin' to some about tryin' to get hold of some land of my own and, well, seein' as how you have so much, and it's so much work, I thought maybe you could give me the land I been workin'. So's I could make a little money for myself. You know, have some things for the family and all."

Mary thought again of all she had given him. His work was not as good as the other share-croppers' and she had often felt he wasn't sharing equally as they had agreed. She didn't like him, but she felt warmth for his wife. His sons greeted her every day with respect.

"What kind of things do you speak of?"

"Well, special things. Things only money can buy. The traders come by carryin' all sorts of things. Things for the wife, maybe."

Mary thought for a moment. She was certainly willing to give to family. She had built a house for her daughter, Nancy, and reserved land for her younger two daughters. She had divided her land for her sons and their families.

"I am able, if I wish, to give or sell my land. But I make no deals without my friend Mr. Jones."

"Aye, I heard tell he handles things for ya, but most say he'll be gone for a while yet. Mr. Parrish helped me draw up the paper. All legal. I have it right here."

He handed her the paper, but she handed it right back.

129

"I have seen no letters of your language for almost sixty springs."

"Oh. Oh, that's right. Well, it just says you'll be giving me forty acres, the ones I been workin' on, free and clear. No more. No less. Your brothers agree, me bein' kin and all. Your brothers say it's your way to share."

She was surprised her Seneca brothers had agreed to give another white man more land. She felt it must have been out of respect for her and she could only reciprocate.

"If my brothers believe it is just, I can not disagree. But only if the paper shows forty acres, the acres we spoke of. No more, as you say, and no less."

George anxiously pointed to the paper.

"Says so right here. See those numbers? That there say forty."

Mary tried to search his eyes for deception. She looked at the paper and tried desperately to remember her English alphabet. It had been too long. With no instruction or practice. She spoke English the same as many of her Seneca family, but she had been denied reading or learning.

"Then I will make my mark. A Seneca lives by truth. You have lived among us for more than two harvests. I have no reason to doubt you." She made her mark and George quickly stuffed the paper in his pocket. He nervously put on his hat and hurried away.

Children, Seneca, white and some a mixture that no one would ever know, ran to Mary's waiting smile. She was always pleased to see them. They danced around her, taking her hand to dance with them. They laughed, and she laughed. She pointed her finger as a signal for them to wait, then she rushed inside her house. She could hear them giggling in anticipation. This was a daily game, now. More and more settlers were building in the villages around the Seneca. Some were wealthy, most were poor and struggling. To Mary the children were special spirits. They'd come running from the forest, the gorge, the fields, always laughing, always naturally in tune with the nature around them. She enjoyed their realness. They wore no masks to her.

She emerged from her house with honey and berries and she with her young spirits shared the sweetness of the season.

Even twenty years later, when those children had grown, they sent their own children to her for berries and honey. She had stayed healthy and continued working in her fields, pounding corn, milking her cow and mending clothes. When the children came, she still danced with them, but not as fast, and sometimes she had to squint as she watched them leave her. Her own children were grown, with grandchildren for her care. Though John was shunned by many Seneca for his killing of another Indian, his children were welcome. Jesse's children were not as fair-haired as he, but they were as gentle. Often Mary ate alone, now. Friends visited, and many a passing settler, having heard of her as The White Woman, came in curious respect to pay her a visit.

The river she so greatly loved had been renamed the Genesee, which, she heard, still meant beautiful valley. The villages around her were changing into large white settlements.

As she sat in her longhouse eating alone she heard the familiar trotting of a horse and smiled. She rose and waited with open arms for her visitor to enter. When he did she made sure her smile would show and her warmth for him beam out from her as the sun. Horatio Jones was her closest friend, her greatest counsel. Though much older now, he, too, still could ride the trails and roads with speed and he never seemed to tire. His smile was special to her and, as he entered, it was the first thing she looked for.

"Mary. I've so missed your company!"

131

"And I yours, Mr. Jones! Sit. Eat. Tell me your stories."

Jones sat on the floor and took some food from the ever present pot.

"Stories about you are all I've been hearin'. Every white man from here to the Ohio, and even beyond that, now, wants to meet the White Woman of The Genesee. Story is you give a cake to every settler that passes through."

Mary smiled. "Missed one once. Heard he and his family came through here when the moon was high. Told some they were in a hurry to go to Buffalo."

"Well, he must be the only white man in the country who didn't get one of your cakes."

"He got one."

"But, you said . . ."

"When I heard he got by me, I cooked up a bunch of those cakes and headed for Buffalo. Walked all the way, same as usual. When I finally got there I asked some folks where the new settler was and they told me he was stayin' in some house near a place called Black Rock. So I went. I saw a wagon full of mud and knew I was in the right place. I walked in while he was sleepin'. And I laid out all those cakes on a cloth right beside him."

"So. He got a bunch?"

"Nope. He heard me startin' to leave and got afraid of my large presence. . . ."

She smiled and twinkled her eyes at Jones and he laughed.

". . . Jumped right up in his nakedness and started yellin'. 'Thieves! Indians! Robbers!' Jumped right up on those little cakes, jumpin' up and down like he was standin' on a nest of bees! Well, turned out only one cake survived. He got it."

Jones laughed hard and shook his head in amazement. She enjoyed his laughter and cherished their sharing of stories. She pretended to get quite serious and watched his face for the right reaction.

"Had to get him that cake," she said. She paused and waited for Jones to question her. He questioned only with his eyes.

"It was my birthday!"

They both laughed then, rocking and laughing and touching each other as good friends do. When they settled down Mary saw Jones' curious look and motioned to him to ask whatever he wanted.

"Which birthday was it?"

"Ah. By Seneca terms I have only one. But the settlers who have flocked to our land like to have frolics. So, we figured out I must be close to eighty now. That new man went sneakin' by here and missed the party!"

"There's no one I enjoy visiting more than I do you, Mary. I wish I could come more often."

They shared their silent agreement for a moment, then Jones looked at her sadly.

"I wish I had been here when your cousin George pulled his deal."

Mary's smile also turned to sadness, but it was more an angry sadness.

"I'm sorry, Mary. Four hundred is sure a lot more than forty. And the scoundrel knew it!"

"It wasn't for you to know, Mr. Jones. It was business between him and me. It was no fault of yours."

It had taken Mary four years to discover the treachery of her cousin, and even then it was by accident. She remembered the day she was about to give a small piece of land to a man who had done a favor for Jesse. She went to the north field to tell George he would have a new neighbor, and to ask him to be kind to the stranger as a favor to her. George tried to chase her away with a rake, shouting that the land she was standing on was his. Cornplanter and Black Coals heard her story and they helped her remove him from the land. Then she heard that he wasn't a cousin. Her father called him cousin because he was the son of a friend. George forever said he was a cousin because he hoped for an inheritance of some kind.

Mary wondered how people could live such lies for the

sake of money or land. She didn't understand why people didn't realize that nature had all the power. That no matter how much land or money a person had, nature always had the upper hand. Land unattended by people would fill itself with plants and animals, and would destroy all reminders that man had once been there. George was a true liar, and a poor thief. She last heard that he was heading some place South, some place called Pitts-Burg.

Jones finished eating and crossed his legs facing Mary. Mary did the same and faced him. This is how they always transacted business. It was their signal to each other that story time was over.

"Well, I'm sorry for the whole deal, anyway. Especially since I'm here to buy up the rest of your land."

"Not all of it, Horatio Jones. I wish to save one tract for me and my family that follows me. By your terms a tract one mile wide and two miles deep."

"I know. I know. And it will be that way, I promise. Mr. Brooks has agreed to a price of . . ."

He pulled a paper from his pocket and checked it.

". . . Three thousand dollars. That figures to be about seventeen cents an acre."

"Is that a fair price?"

"Fair as can be!"

"It seems there are many whites around us now. I hear the axes chopping from the first sun."

"That's true. Government's already set up seven reservations just in Seneca country."

"Reservations?"

"Land. Special for the Seneca. Other tribes, too. The government says it's the only way to protect Indian rights."

"Strange protection, my friend. Moving Indians away from their land to put them on government land."

"Oh, no. The reservations are Indian land. To do with as they please. The government will have no say. Forever!"

"Forever?"

"Yep. Forever. So, do we have a deal on this?"

Mary thought about all the white people around her, how their ways were so different from the Seneca. She thought of the crops and the high price of trading. Her family needed the money. Hunting ground and farm lands weren't as lush as they once were. She looked at the paper in Jones' hand and felt she was looking at what was left of a nation. The grandeur of the Seneca, of the Six Nations, reduced to a small piece of paper.

Sadly she answered. "Let it be so."

Jones put the paper away as a young Seneca woman entered the house and looked at Mary. Mary motioned for her to join them at the fire. The woman went to the fire, but instead of sitting, took ashes from it, as Mary had once done, and smeared them on the outside of Mary's door.

Mary rose slowly, looked at the ashes, at Jones, at the ashes. She touched the ashes with her hand as someone touches a beloved child.

"Who travels from my heart?"

The Seneca woman answered her. "John . . ."

Mary grabbed at her heart, gasping.

". . . And . . . Jesse."

Mary was frozen in anguish and disbelief. She held herself up in the door frame as warriors brought the bodies of her sons to her. Jones went to her side to console her, but she held him away. This grief was the kind only a mother could feel. It couldn't be shared. Silently, slowly she went to her sons.

It was Jesse she went to first. Carefully she cupped his cheek, as she had done so long ago. Her head tilted, her wrinkled face unable to form an expression, she gently brushed back the blond hair of her son, fixed the collar on his white man's jacket, and gasped in the breath of grief.

She turned to John and touched him with her fingertips. She nodded her head, forgiving him for all he had done in the best. She understood him, now. He was John. She had stopped trying to change him long ago. He wasn't meant to be happy. The world had changed around him too quickly. The nature of things had spun against him. She understood. She forgave.

More Seneca gathered as she again went to Jesse. All the love and life in her soul felt ripped from her body. She bent to kiss him and felt her emptiness as Black Coals came to her.

"White man's whiskey has stolen more of your family."

Mary could see he didn't like the job of messenger. His love for her showed in his eyes and she tried to make it easier by softening to him.

"John killed Jesse while they gathered the white man's lumber."

Mary looked at him with emptiness. She hadn't imagined that Jesse's death was from John's hand.

"John felt lowly before his Creator. He was jealous of your love for Jesse, angered at Jesse's whiteness. He wished to tell you of his sorrow. But he, too, was killed. By Mohawk who shared his bottle. They will be punished by the council fire."

Mary bowed her head at the news and Black Coals touched her warmly on the arm. Three Seneca women came through the crowd and Mary greeted them with sorrow.

"Come, my daughters. Say good-bye and send your brothers on their journey."

CONCLUSION

12

Mary buried John with full Seneca dignity and tradition. In spite of her contempt for him for his deadly acts against her family, he was still her son. She placed a cake on the skins next to him, just as she had done with Hiokatoo. Jesse was given a white man's funeral and buried closer to Tom. Some time before their deaths, she had remembered baby Jane who died at birth, and she had made a marker for her so all would remember.

The graves were all solid now. It had been five years since her sons' death and Mary came every day to remove the weeds and straighten the markers.

"Truman Stone! It has been long since I have seen you! Join me!"

Truman Stone was a leader among the many white settlers in the valley and he often visited Mary to tell her stories or bring her news.

"Mrs. Jemison, I come with your neighbors."

He led her outside her longhouse to face a sea of people. She knew some of them. As she eyed the crowd she moved curiously closer.

"My eyes are not what they used to be, Mr. Stone." Stone let her put her arm in his as she greeted her friends. Most were smiling and silent. Some wiped away a tear or looked shyly to the ground.

"What is it, Mr. Stone? Are they sick? Are they ailing?"

"They've come in celebration."

"Celebration? Is this is a white man's holiday that I've somehow missed?"

The crowd opened and formed a path for Mary as Stone led her by them. She smiled and nodded, humble but regal, and took Stone's lead to a large table covered with adorned packages, carvings, teas and herbs, blankets and a large present wrapped in purple paper.

"They're here to celebrate you, Mrs. Jemison."

Stone stepped a few feet away as a young German woman made her way to the front. She approached the table and picked up a package of ginseng tea, then shyly, stood to face Mary.

"Mrs. Jemison. Once my husband came to you by accident and you greeted him at your door with warmth and a cup of tea. You went to your loft and found the last of your stored food to give to him and the rest of my family. When he offered to pay with what little he had, you told him no. We ate through the winter because of you. My husband's dead now, and my children grown. All I have to give is this tea."

She handed it to Mary and tried to back away, but Mary held her hand until the old woman would look her in the eye.

"We'll share this tea on a journey some day," Mary said. "It will warm us both."

The old woman smiled proudly and went back to the crowd.

A tall husky man of forty stepped forward next and carried a pile of wooden bowls, spoons and ladles. Mary squinted and tried to remember him. He laid the wooden implements at her feet, removed his brimmed hat and smiled broadly.

"Ah! It's Mr. Fawcett! You've grown some over the years!"

"That I have, Ma'am."

He stood next to Mary and spoke to the crowd.

"I'm here to tell ya 'bout a time I was almost dead. Seems like it wasn't long ago, but it was more than ten years. Well,

140

Mrs. Jemison here heard tell I was sick and ready to breathe my last. She took my young son Davy into the woods beyond her flats and showed him some things about finding herbs. On the stormiest night ever in these parts I opened my eyes to the nicest smile I ever did see . . . next to my wife's, of course. Well, Mrs. Jemison, she had stayed up all night grinding those herbs in a wooden bowl and putting them on my feet, my head . . . most anywhere you can think of."

He wrapped an arm around a much smaller Mary and roughly drew her close to him.

"Well, I'm here to tell ya, or show you, I guess, that I'm here. And this here woman done her best to make that happen."

He squeezed her again and beamed at the people. Mary pushed him away gently before he cracked any of her bones, but she smiled back with pride at the life she helped save.

Another man stepped forward and gave her a carved walking stick.

"In case you ever need it," he said.

Still another came with a blanket full of color.

"To replace the one you gave me five winters back."

A little curly haired boy of five or so stepped to her next, and Mary bent to be more on his level.

"Mrs. Jemison?"

The boy's lower lip quivered and a large covered bowl shook in his hands. Mary knew him well.

"What is it, little James?"

She raised his chin to look at her and she could see the purple and red juice covering his mouth and cheeks. James looked down ashamed and Mary understood.

"No need for shame, young James. The Creator put those berries here for us to enjoy."

She cupped his chin again and smiled lovingly.

"I'm glad you tasted them for me first. Were they good?"

James nodded. Mary could see he felt better.

"Good. I feel better now, do you?"

James hugged her and started to cry.

"What is it, boy? Have I done something wrong?"

"No. I mean, no, Ma'am."

"Then what is it?"

"I want you to be my grandma." He stepped back, his tears mixing with his juicy cheeks and eyes pleading.

"Can you, please? Can you be my grandma?"

Mary searched the crowd for his mother who nodded proudly.

"I think I'd be proud to be your grandma, little James. Except for one thing."

"Yes, ma'am?"

"You have to promise, an Indian promise, that you won't eat all the berries in my valley."

"Oh, yes, ma'am!"

James hugged her again and ran back to his mother. He had forgotten to leave the bowl, so he ran back to Mary and handed it to her. The people laughed. And the people cried.

For more than an hour they came and honored her. When there was but one present left on the table Mr. Stone again took over.

"There is one gift left for you, Mrs. Jemison, but I'm afraid the giver is a little late. Would you like to open it, or save it?"

"No need to wait."

Mary knew the voice and her excitement showed as she opened her arms to Horatio Jones.

"It's been many years, Mr. Jones."

She held back the tears that wanted to push themselves out. So much love overwhelmed her. Jones took the package from the table and held it for Mary to open.

"I don't really know how you'll feel about this, Mrs. Jemison. I tried to fix it up special, knowin' how much it means to you. I didn't take the old one, just used it so's I could copy it. If you don't like it I suppose I could always, I don't know, maybe change it or somethin', to make it better, I mean, that is, to make it more . . ."

"Horatio, shut up!"

Mary carefully tore the purple paper and opened it while Jones waited sheepishly next to her. The crowd murmured and "ooed" and "ahed" as she lifted the gift from the paper. Mary's heart felt as though it would explode as she smoothed the wood and smelled the oak.

"You did fine work, Mr. Jones. It is perfect."

She raised the gift for the crowd to see and proudly displayed it.

"Mr. Jones has made a perfect copy of my first cradle board, one cherished by me, as also this shall be."

The carving and the painting were exactly as Sheninjee had done. She was sure Sheninjee would be pleased and the tears from Mary's eyes flowed freely. She lowered the board, cradled it in front of her, and the crowd broke into spontaneous applause. She had loved Sheninjee, cherished his gentleness. Horatio's gift to her was as strong as any wampum belt for it gave her the promise of an inner peace that all Seneca long for.

13

Jones joined her as she said her last goodbye to the graves of her children. She straightened her now gray hair that hung almost to her waist, then wrapped it in as tight a bun as she could.

"You're as beautiful as when I first saw ya," Jones said. She had done her job of growing old and done it well. Though her back was curved and her head slightly bent so that she often peeked from under her eyebrows, her face had not changed. Her eyes still glistened with life, her white teeth still lit the way of her smile and only a bit of rosiness was missing from her cheeks.

"I'm sad to see you go," Jones said. This land won't seem the same without you tending it."

Together they gazed at the gorge and Jones put a gentle hand on Mary's shoulder. A white family rode by in their wagon and the children waved to Mary. She nodded and smiled, but Jones felt her shudder.

"I feel sorry for them," she said.

"Feel sorry? For them? Mary, I don't understand you. You've been Seneca longer than most of these people been alive. White people conquered the Seneca, destroyed the Iroquois nation and you stand here feeling sorry?"

Mary turned to face him and stood proudly as she spoke.

"You are wrong, Mr. Jones. The Seneca have not been conquered. And the Iroquois will endure. The people you see here, the white people, they are the ones who feel destruction. They come to this new land and spend their lives searching for their homes. The Irish try to be like the English; the English like the French. They've lost their homes, their culture. They are not at peace with nature or each other. They chop the trees to build walls. They hunt and let the meat spoil. They will always fight. They will always hate. Does the bear live with the wolf and follow the ways of the wolf? Does the turtle race with the deer? White people will spend their time trying to be like each other and making others like them. They will never find a home here. This land was not discovered, Mr. Jones. It was created. And all things on it are gifts from the Creator. The Seneca were not conquered. The Seneca and their land have been dishonored. Someday white people will come to us and ask us how to live here, how to honor the land and those who share it. The Seneca will be here. The Iroquois nation will be here to answer."

They stood silently. Then Mary donned her burden strap and squeezed Jones' arm. As she walked away quietly, he called to her.

"What little money there is for the last piece of land will go to the Nation, as you wish it to be. Go well, my friend."

14

Mary made her walk to her new home. She had tired of the white people's ways and longed for the spirits of the Seneca. Though she loved the settlers for the tributes they had paid to her, there were many times and many things she could not accept about them. She needed Indian values and Indian tradition to sustain her. She sent her daughters ahead to the reservation at Buffalo Creek and, after many days of walking, she found the area near the waters of Erie. A sign was by a road that seemed to her to be an entrance. She looked at it, but she couldn't read it. She continued down the road until a Seneca woman finally greeted her.

"Come! You are Mary? Nancy's mother?"

Mary nodded and opened her arms in grateful welcome.

"Is this the place they call Buffalo Creek? The special land?"

"Yes. Buffalo Creek."

"I've come to live with my people."

The young woman took a bag from Mary's hand and led Mary down the road.

"Then, you are home," she said.

They walked past small, run-down houses and fields that were mostly weed. Another small house, built better than the others, had a small sign on it.

"Why are there so many signs? In a Seneca village?"

"Missionaries. And the government. The ones of green

and yellow are government signs. They are here to tell us which way to come and go."

"What do they say?"

"Don't know. Only the people of the government can read them."

Mary twinkled her eyes at the young girl.

"They must be the ones who are lost," Mary said.

The girl continued. "The signs of red are missionary signs. For those who wish to follow the Christian way of God."

"Oh. So, they're lost, too."

Mary settled in an old cabin not far from her daughters. They were married now, with children to worry about. She spent much of her time alone. The fields were no good for planting. The government had put up something called a dam which stole the water from the Seneca. She had no money. The small annual payments that Horatio Jones sent her went mostly for food.

She slept on the floor of her cabin and it was there the missionaries always found her when they came to visit. One woman in particular had come to visit her every day for weeks. Mary didn't really pay any attention to what she was saying. She just enjoyed the company.

But today she didn't want the woman to come. She lay on the floor awaking from a bad dream. A dream that took her back to her farm and family. It made her body hurt and she wasn't sure she could be kind. She heard the woman outside and waited. When the missionary entered, Mary feigned sleep. But the woman stood there patiently, as if her presence was enough of an alarm to wake anyone, including the dead.

Mary gave up. She acted surprised and excited that the woman was there. She motioned for her to sit on the floor, which the woman did reluctantly. Mary looked at the bible in the woman's hand and remembered her dream. She tapped her lip, waiting for the missionary to begin her daily speech.

"Mrs. Jemison. I came to continue our talks of yesterday. To help you repent. To be saved,"

Mary smiled an impish smile.

"Saved? Saved? What is it again that I'm being saved from?"

"Why, your sins, of course. To repent. To be saved."

Mary continued playing.

"Oh. My sins. How?"

"How?"

"How?"

"How, what?"

"How will I be saved?"

"By accepting the Lord, of course. As we spoke of yesterday."

Now Mary understood why she was having the nightmares about her past. She stopped tapping her lip and got very solemn.

"Don't know what you mean about being saved. I've tried to live good. I've never done anything against your God or the Great Creator. I've been dragged almost to your hell, and I've been tempted daily. But my mother and father have always been with me. Am I afraid to die? I am not! Am I afraid of being hungry? At this age I hunger. Am I sorry for the death of my Tom? For the murder of my Jesse? Or the just killing of my John? Will accepting your God change that? Saved. Saved? I am not afraid to die."

Mary succeeded in embarrassing and frustrating the young missionary. She felt sorry for her. She guessed she wasn't really as zealous as she seemed. She was doing a job that she felt important.

Mary busied herself preparing for her final path. Confidant and sure that the remainder of her children were happy and well-cared for, she decided to appease whatever God might be in charge of her fate. Though she was faithful to the

Great Creator of her Seneca people, she didn't trust that the white man's God might not still have a say in her life. Faithful that her Creator wouldn't mind, she attended the missionary school on the reservation and learned again the prayers of her parents. As if fate or God or the Creator had listened, she died at the age of ninety-one, one month after reaccepting the God of the White man.

She was buried as a white woman, on the reservation, near a corn field. An old man on crutches carved a wooden marker for her grave. Her people planted a black walnut tree in remembrance of her strength. Some time later her body was returned to the beautiful valley. A branch from her tree was planted to grow with her memory and a statue erected in her likeness. The inscription reads:

Mrs. Mary Jemison
The White Woman of the Genesee

EPILOGUE

The life of Mrs. Mary Jemison has inspired numerous books loosely based on the story of this remarkable individual. Mary's true story, depicted in this book, is more interesting than fictional accounts which have attempted to portray a similar character. I am an eighth-generation descendant of this Scotch-Irish woman born on the high seas while her parents were crossing from Ireland to America. About ten years ago I decided to document my family genealogy and so I began with my father. He helped me to reconstruct five generations. Two elderly women then living on the Cattaraugus Reservation provided the names which took me back to the sixth generation. Then working forward from Mary I believe I've identified the son, Tom, from whom my family got the Jemison name. He was from Mary's first marriage to Sheninjee, a Delaware Indian. Tom married four times. By his third wife, a Seneca woman (whose name we do not know), he had a son, George. George Jemison was my grandfather.

The life story of Mary contains many lessons. Through them I have come to understand the tragedies and triumphs which she knew. Her adoption into the Seneca Nation was a blessing which she came to appreciate when she was old enough to understand it. Adoption in the 18th century meant something more than an Indian name; it included rights and responsibilities which Seneca women inherited at birth, for we are a matrilineal society. She was fortunate to have a husband who was a good provider and figure of strength. He looked after her and their children and together they spent 50 years living next to the Genesee River. Through her words we learn how the Sullivan Campaign of burn and destroy impacted upon Seneca people. Mary survived the terrible winter of 1779–80 because of two escaped slaves and their generosity. She and her five children were given refuge in the home of these two African-Americans, within Seneca territory, beyond the reach of the American Army and its path of total destruction. The irony of African slaves believing they are protecting a white woman from the Senecas, when it is the American Army that she is fleeing, could not have been imagined by a Hollywood writer.

The third major theme that emerges is the terrible toll which alcoholism took upon her family. To lose her favorite son, who was murdered by his brother while drunk, is a lesson for everyone to observe. The damage wrought by alcohol was further illustrated by the tragic events of recent days on the Cattaraugus Reservation when a political struggle escalated into an armed confrontation which left three men dead. Emotions fueled by alcohol lead to tragic results. Our Seneca prophet, Handsome Lake, referred to alcohol as the "mind changer."

Mary lived a long and sometimes difficult life, but her story is a testament to the triumph of the human spirit. Though small in stature, she was mighty in the determined way she lived.

G. Peter Jemison
Historic Site Manager,
Ganondagan State Historic Site,
Victor, New York